CARIBBEAN

BONES

TALES FROM A PARADISE LOST

CARIBBEAN

BONES

TALES FROM A PARADISE LOST

RICHARD CORWIN

Bujew
Press

Caribbean Bones

This is a work of fiction. Names, characters, places and
incidents either are the product of the author's imagination or are used fictitiously, and any resemblance to any
actual persons, living or dead, events or locales is entirely
coincidental.

1st Edition published by Richard Corwin
ISBN-13: 978-1466252585
ISBN-10: 1466252588

To order additional copies of this book please contact:
corwinshome@yahoo.com or bujewpress@gmail.com

Cover Silhouette Image by Barbara Behune
Book and Cover design by Tom Crockett

Printed in the United States of America

Acknowledgments

Some people come into our lives and quickly go. Some stay for a while, leave footprints on our hearts, and we are never, ever the same.

Flavia Weedn

Caribbean Bones began several years ago in Florida when I wrote my first short story for Caribe News and Reviews. At the time I had no idea that I would write anything more than the one story of my time in the islands but with encouragement from friends the book was born. I think they were tired of listening to my endless tales of how life was there when it was easy, simple, relaxed, fun, adventurous, and exciting.

My wife Brenda means more to the books completion than as a casual reader or critique. She provided an in depth analysis, where experts failed at great expense, to unveil the manuscripts strengths, weaknesses and necessary corrections to put meat on the stories bones. She is responsible if the book succeeds in attracting the interest of readers.

The Chesapeake Bay Writers group in Williamsburg was subjected to me reading many of the stories and urged completion of *Caribbean Bones* for the better part of four years but like many writers I had to rewrite each story until they were so over cooked that I had to start over.

I dedicate the book to my friends in the islands who may still be alive and well. I want them to know how much I owe them for the memories, good times, and absolute joy of being in their company but especially their contributions to *Caribbean Bones*. John and Phyllis Gawker were special friends I knew in Virginia before the idea to locate in St. Thomas ever occurred to me. When they moved to the islands and encouraged me to visit, it began my decade's long life in paradise and to them I am especially grateful; they made my dreams and *Caribbean Bones* possible.

Richard Corwin
2011

The test of an adventure is that when you're in the middle of it, you say to yourself, "Oh, now I've got myself into an awful mess; I wish I were sitting quietly at home." And the sign that something's wrong with you is when you sit quietly at home wishing.

Thornton Wilder 1897-1975,
American Novelist, and Playwright.

CONTENTS

INTRODUCTION

We should come home from adventures, and perils, and discoveries every day with new experience and character.

Henry David Thoreau

White capped seas, twenty feet; some higher with howling winds in excess of forty knots, sunless grey skies, and dark moonless nights, made the first days of our voyage exhausting. It was during one of those dark, sleepless nights, with wind screaming through the rigging and waves crashing over the boat, that Dave, who was struggling to control the boat, told us what to do if it became necessary to abandon ship; six hundred miles from the nearest shore. Henry would grab the water and small bag of provisions; Richard and Olin, release the two life rafts and Dave, as last one off, would grab the ditch bag with passports, and emergency gear.

That was the fourth night out as waves were sweeping over the boat, into the cockpit and soaking my bunk. The newly installed single side band radio quit working on the first day. Without a working radio, we had no warning that we were sailing into tropical storm Ida; a storm that would damage several boats and cause extensive damage along the Virginia coast. It had been a few years since I had done any blue water sailing; especially in weather like that and was not prepared for anything but mild sea sickness.

The voyage began when my friend Dave, who had listened to my stories of years living and sailing in the islands, asked me to go along as crew.

I got to the boat the day before the race as Dave and Henry were busy making last minute preparations; stowing provisions, adding a new single side band radio, securing fuel tanks to the deck, and making sure all through-hull fittings had proper plugs in the event one failed. The next morning we followed the racing fleet into the Bay.

Dave had entered the Crystal Spray, a fifty-two foot Jeanneau, in the Caribbean 1500 rally that began on a cold November morning in the choppy waters of the Chesapeake Bay. We would be sailing with a fleet of other boats in the annual race to Sopers Hole and Nanny Cay in Tortola. As it neared the starting time, the cluster of sails fluttered like nervous sea gulls near the committee boat; nervously waiting for the signal to begin the race.

I was overjoyed to be sailing again after so many years; especially back to a place that meant so much to me. Sailing across the Atlantic was more physically challenging than sailing on the James River and riskier, but I was in good shape for my age and the adventure of ocean sailing always appealed to me.

Explorations of jungle cities had been my life's passion but I found sailing in the open ocean a different form of exploration. Both had the challenge of overcoming loneliness and overcoming dangerous conditions with a cool head. This trip sail back to the islands was something I always wanted to do and when offered the chance, I couldn't wait to leave.

At noon the race was officially under way and the Crystal Spray lunged forward, digging her bow deep into the cold, gray waves. She heeled over starboard rail just a few inches above the water as the rigging complained loudly.

Within a few hours, we passed over the Chesapeake Bay Bridge tunnel and pushed out of the Bay into the chilly high seas of the ocean, quickly losing sight of other boats in the rough seas.

I had sailed along this part of the ocean several times before but now it was very different; several decades had come and gone making my expectations difficult and very personal. I was returning to a place that had been my home for many years, a place of great joy and fond memories; a paradise then but now, after so many years, I knew it the island would not be the same. They would be a victim of their own popularity; polluted beaches, overdeveloped by greedy land owners, sewerage dumped into the ocean by fleets of charter yachts and dead or dying reefs.

Now, after almost a week of foul weather, high seas, sea sickness, damaged gear, wet bunk, and making repairs, we were nearing the end of the race. When we neared Puerto Rico, the weather calmed, seas began to flatten, and my watch was nearing an end.

On the horizon small dark shapes appeared then grew larger revealing clusters of islands. As we approached we

3

tried to identify what islands we were seeing. Jost van Dyke, Thatch Island, and Tortola appeared. The water slowly changed from a rich dark blue of deep water to electric neon blue as the water became shallow.

At the sighting of the islands I felt an ache of anticipation like being stricken by love for the very first time. It was a strange mixture of emotions; a fear of seeing changes with an overwhelming and reserved excitement of returning to a home I loved so much. And made more troubling was suppressing a feeling I would be tempted to stay.

There was plenty for me to remember and lots I had forgotten. Four decades is a lot to reflect on; a lot of memories to dredge up. The Crystal Spray, pushed by gentle winds, sliced almost noiselessly through the water. Under sail, the soft, early morning Caribbean breeze kept the boat cool and tropical heat ashore. Dave ran out all the sails he had on board as we neared Jost Van Dyke. It was important, approaching the end of the trip into Sopers Hole, that we were seen with all sails up.

I looked for some recognizable landmarks from my past but there were none. Even Cane Garden Bay was developed beyond recognition but memories did come back with a rush, like the howling of the early morning winds and high seas of just a few days ago. I was overwhelmed with emotion, unable to keep away the tears or the swelling in my throat. I became painfully aware of the dramatic changes as we sailed past the island with new homes and condos clustered around the beaches and along once lush green hillsides.

After dinner and a nights rest in Sopers Hole we sailed to Nanny Cay, where the Caribbean 1500 boats gathered to celebrate the end of the race. It wasn't until I reached St. Thomas that the full impact of change hit me.

The ferry landed and my first look at St. Thomas, unlike decades before, was it had the appearance of Miami, the traffic of New York City and crime of Los Angeles. Expensive condos and hotel lights spread an eerie Las Vegas-like, abnormal glow over the ocean at night.

Missing were the colorful blue, red and white island native schooners that years ago crowded the dock along the town's waterfront selling conch, fish, chickens, fruit, vegetables, and other cargo. The spectacle of island paradise living was gone.

I raced to the airport unable to ignore the ugly mega cruise ships that loomed over the nearby buildings and traffic. I arrived at the modern Cyril King airport that had replaced the decade's old, rustic and friendly Harry S. Truman airport.

I looked around and remembered the old field house terminal; Jean and Larry's airport bar no longer there to hang out in; no more goats or chickens or donkeys wandering freely. This new airport, like every other busy airport in the world, was coldly efficient, sterile and friendless. No individuality, lots of traffic, a small snack bar serving micro-waved sandwiches and portion controlled, machine dispensed coffee. Intimacy was something of the past.

After hours of waiting and long security lines I finally stumbled into the waiting area where a sea of passengers were shopping in the typical free port gift shops hawking T shirts, ball caps and pretty much the same cheap, Chinese made stuff available at every other airport in the world.

With little sleep for two weeks I spread out on several waiting room padded chrome chairs, propped up against a concrete pillar and quickly fell asleep on my bags. Awakened by the announcement my flight was boarding, I had some regrets at not taking the time I spent sitting in the airport to tour the town. Just as well, I thought, it would have been depressing. It was best to leave and remember the island the way it was; remember this was once truly a paradise and the Caribbean frontier where I made extraordinary friends and met remarkable people.

TWO TOKES TO TAKE OFF

One way to get the most out of life is to look upon it as an adventure.

William Feather

Dick Chandler's Paradise began in a tired looking World War II surplus DC-3. Dick was on his way to fulfill a dream he had of living in the Caribbean and couldn't have planned a better way to get there. For the moment his joy was being in the old plane. It didn't matter it was a lot smaller, louder, and far less comfortable than the Pan Am jet to San Juan. Discovering his own Shangri-La was getting closer; his heart beat faster and like a man going to his wedding, who couldn't wait to get his long awaited reward, Dick sat on the edge of his small seat impatiently urging the pilot to go faster. The old plane was in keeping with his idea of a rugged, no frills trip he expected. After unforeseen delays of leaving the states, he was on his way to the place he had dreamed of for such a long time; the Caribbean to explore the islands, do some sailing, scuba diving, and maybe a little treasure hunting.

The planes air-conditioning system, a few small fans evenly spaced on the overhead luggage racks, labored frantically as if they would shake loose at any minute, to circulate the warm, sticky, salt air inside the stuffy cabin. Sweat streamed down the back of Dick's neck, down his face, through his beard, soaking the front of his shirt and blue jeans; long sleeves rolled up in an effort to get cool. Outside, the roar of the two large oil streaked Rolls-Royce engines reduced conversations to sign language, lip reading, or simple nods.

A passenger sitting next to Dick pointed to a small island below. Shouting over the roar of the plane's engine he said it was called Sail Rock; St. Thomas wasn't far now; they'd be landing soon. While looking out the small window he saw the ocean slowly change from a cold deep blue to a brighter neon blue as the water became shallower; a sure sign they were nearing the islands. Below, sail boats left trails of bluish-white foam in their wakes and he watched trance-like until they disappeared out of view; thinking of the day when he would be sailing; maybe get lucky enough to have his own boat.

Soon he would be landing in a strange place where he knew nothing more than what little he had seen and read about in magazines; a little nervous but eager to see the familiar faces of his old friends John and Phyllis who had moved to St. Thomas several years before and were now living aboard their own boat.

Suddenly, and without warning, the engines roar became a loud, deep, throaty groan and, as if protesting the unexpected change, the plane shuddered violently like it would shake apart when the flaps were extended and landing gear fell into place. The props feathered and the plane began a steep, rapid, ear popping descent into the Harry S. Truman airport. After a couple of rough bounces the plane taxied to the gate, jerked to a stop, the door opened, and he retrieved his duffel bag from the overhead luggage rack. He followed the crew and pilot and stepped into a new world of tropical heat that smelled and felt like the exciting paradise he hoped for.

It didn't take long to work up more sweat as he de-planed into the mid-afternoon tropics; his cool weather clothing out of place and now soaking wet. He looked at the cream colored post war airport terminal; rust streaked down its overly painted sides from old fittings. Its rustic cluttered, unorganized building made him feel that he was truly on a new and great unknown adventure; a few goats, Canary donkeys and chickens wandered aimlessly around the airport fences and goose bumps erupted on the pale skin of his arms; cheeks flushed with excitement as more sweat ran down his neck and back causing his heavy clothing to stick to his skin.

Unlike Florida or Virginia, the island's air, although hot, felt free of oppressive humidity and stifling heat. He was happy to be on solid ground, took a deep breath then walked toward the crude terminal building; a one time hanger. Typical of most other airports was the bustling taxi stands; ticket counters for smaller plane charters, hotel posters and noticeably absent were rental cars. He later learned that taxi drivers had a union strong enough to keep the business of rental cars off the island; most taxis were owned by island government employees and that included the governor's staff.

The terminal was surrounded by small chain link fencing and flimsy gates that only directed boarding and arriving passengers—no international quarantines in 1963.

Once through the gate Dick stopped long enough to rearrange his grip on his bag and step around a couple of chickens darting carefully between people's feet. Standing next to him, on the other side of the fence, was a man he recognized from his flight. He rolled, and lit a rather large joint.

"Have a toke?" he asked, "Best damn Jamaican you can ever smoke. "He said handing it to Dick; he was understandably nervous, but couldn't refuse. "Thanks," He took a deep drag, coughed a few times and handed it back.

"See that mountain?" The stranger pointed to a large mountain at the far end of the runway. "When you fly outta' here you gotta' go over that and that makes me very nervous so I smoke at least two of these before flyin' outta here." They passed the joint back and forth until it was gone.

Dick looked at the mountain; at the runway and could see his point. The plane would have to be at full throttle with a tail wind before starting down the runway to clear the mountain. (Years later the government removed the mountain top after several planes failed to clear it).

He lit another joint, took a couple of hits and handed it to Dick who stepped to one side to let some people pass. "Sounds like you fly quite a bit," Dick said squinting into the bright sunlight to look at the mountain.

"Every Goddamn day, and every Goddamn day I smoke at least two Jamaicans before leaving."

"So, why fly so much?" Dick asked still looking at the

short runway and mountain. He inhaled deeply a second time on the new joint, choked a couple of times, and handed it back. "You're not the pilot, are you? "

"Yep. I'm the pilot," he said matter-of-factly, took one last, long puff then handed it back to Dick. "Keep it." He said before strolling off to his plane waiting to return to Puerto Rico. Dick thought, almost aloud, "at least he'll be happier than the passengers if he hits the mountain."

He watched as the pilot climbed the stairs, closed the door and soon the plane choked to life in a plume of black smoke, engines sputtered then it slowly taxied to the end of the runway preparing for take-off. Grateful the pilot was able to get him here safely, he took one more deep drag on the joint, rubbed away the hot embers, ate what was left, picked up his bag, and walked into the crowded hanger pushing aside determined taxi drivers. At the moment he didn't want a taxi or hotel. The joint made him thirsty and crave an icy Cuba Libre he saw advertised on a Don Q Rum poster inside the terminal; a perfect drink, he thought, after such a long trip.

HARRY S. TRUMAN AIRPORT

To know how to free one self is nothing; the arduous thing is to know what to do with one's freedom.

Andre Gide

Dick wandered around in the terminal until he found a small souvenir gift shop stuffed with tourist guides, maps, paper back books, local newspapers, magazines and racks of brightly colored, cheap airport T-shirts and cases of duty free, imported and domestic cigarettes of all brands. Sitting behind an old cash register was a young, friendly, native girl, filing her nails, who chirped out a birdlike greeting. It was his first time to hear the local island dialect and he was captivated by its romantic inflections. She was surrounded by racks of postcards; stuffed animals wearing miniature St. Thomas "T" shirts hanging from ceiling tiles, and a show case full of cheap glass souvenirs. While gawking curiously at the trinkets, the girl and studying the endless brands of imported cigarettes, he saw what he was looking for. Partially hidden behind cases of liquor and cardboard boxes of cigarettes stacked in a corner, a glass door smeared with sweaty handprints with randomly placed decals on the glass advertising a wide variety of cigarettes, alcohol and beer; the airport lounge.

Dick had smoked the last of his Pall Mall cigarettes during the long flight and now, with so many imported cigarettes to choose from he knew nothing about, he randomly bought an interesting looking carton of imported British Sailor cigarettes. Until he knew better the colorful packaging was the only attraction.

He thanked the girl, stepped around the boxes and pulled the door open not knowing what to expect on the other side. A rush of cold, stale, smoky air swept past him, like ground fog, and up his sweaty pants leaving a cold damp chill on his legs. The dimly lit lounge had an atmosphere that Humphrey Bogart or Sydney Greenstreet would have liked; a place where any self respecting adventurer would be in a dark corner, hatching some nefarious plan under slow moving ceiling fans.

Once his eyes were accustomed to the dark, he found the bar; the one place with light. Against its' back wall glass shelves, filled with odd shaped bottles of every brand of alcohol imaginable, reflected their glassy images in the bars splash board mirror that doubled their numbers. Dick walked carefully to the bar, afraid of bumping into someone, and inspired by the airport posters, ordered a Don Q Rum and coke, with a squeeze of lime; a Cuba Libra. The bartender poured a double shot over ice, mixed with just enough Coke to change the drinks color, coated the edge of the glass with a lime before dropping it into the drink with an explanation that alcohol was cheaper than mixer; "that's why drinks were strong" he said. "You'll get used to it; be careful how many drinks you have."

Gripping his napkin covered glass; Dick thanked him and looked around searching for a place to sit. Slowly his eyes had adjusted to the dimly lit room and through the haze of cigarette smoke saw a comfortable looking, quiet corner booth where he could stretch out and relax after his long trip; maybe get rid of the ringing in his ears caused by sitting so close to the planes roaring engines.

Against the wall an antique Wurlitzer jukebox stood quietly, un-patronized against and alone; its bubbling lava lamp lights cast eerie shafts of colored lights over the bar-room floor penetrating the lingering smog of cigarette smoke. He was grateful it was being ignored. Except for occasional whispers, from somewhere in the shadows, it was a welcomed silence. Dick imagined the few hushed voices could be lovers meeting secretly or maybe some nefarious business deal was being hatched. He preferred to think it was the latter.

The cracked red vinyl seat was soft, compared to the planes upholstery, and it creaked like old leather. His damp clothes were cold, sticky and uncomfortable as he slid cautiously over a patch of loose vinyl repair tape. He propped one leg up on the seat, leaned his head against the wall, closed his eyes, and waited for his body heat to warm up his clothes; for the moment forgetting the Cuba Libre.

Eyes closed, Dick thought back about the events that brought him here to live his dream. With the influence of the Jamaican marijuana still in his system, he was completely relaxed after his long day of traveling. Peaceful images of how he first saw the islands as a true paradise in Yachting Magazine and how they changed the course of his life. He was finally here. The long flight forgotten, his drink unnoticed, tense muscles relaxed and his sweaty clothes ignored. He thought back to his brief stop to visit friends in Florida before continuing on to St. Thomas and wondered how their restaurant, marriage and everything else turned out for them.

When he arrived in Sarasota for a brief visit, his friend Pete talked him into staying just a little longer because he and his girlfriend were finally getting married. Pete lived in a one room apartment above an abandoned carpet store with two day beds placed in opposite corners at one end of the room with a small Pullman kitchen at the other end. There was no privacy but that didn't seem to bother Pete or his girlfriend Sue but Dick found it helpful to smoke several joints if she stayed the night otherwise he wouldn't be able to get much sleep.

Sue's dad had come to town to help with their wedding plans and while there insisted on helping them set up a small business; money was no object. Sue said she would like to have a small restaurant and she had one in mind. Her dad wanted some peace of mind that his daughter would have a future if things didn't work out with Pete and buying her a business was worth the cost; but a restaurant? He knew Pete was a big risk but no matter how hard he tried, he couldn't talk his daughter into canceling the wedding or give up buying a restaurant.

Pete finished in the bathroom, sat on the edge of his bed scratching his crotch, pulled on his socks, lit a joint, coughed then got up to get a beer. Barely awake, Dick took the pillow off his head, rolled over, lit the stub of a joint, and stumbled to the bathroom. He couldn't believe Sue would call before noon knowing they wouldn't be worth a shit after a long night of beer, wine and drugs; their systems weren't ready to function yet and Dick was barely able to understand what Pete was talking about when he told him why Sue had called.

Something about an empty restaurant near the Idle Hour bar and Northside Tavern; her dad had agreed to look at it. Dick vaguely remembered an empty restaurant across the street from the Idle Hour Bar but other than a faint memory, it meant nothing to him. The phone rang again. It was Sue.

Without carpeting, the wood floors caused the phone's ringing to reverberate in the near empty room causing its high pitched tinny bell to annoyingly bounce around the room; not good for a hangover. The phone, like everything else loose in the apartment, was at the far end of the room on an ironing board, covered in dirty laundry, magazines, empty beer bottles; standing between the small kitchen and bathroom like a cheap room divider.

Sue said she was on her way over to the Idle Hour with her dad and wanted them to meet there to look at the vacant restaurant across the street.

Dick couldn't believe she was serious. From what little he remembered the place had been closed for a long time. Apparently Sue told her dad it was a good place for a cheap café or diner near the school and small enough that she could handle it.

George, the owner, was pretty anxious to beat it out of town because his ex wife was after him. Dick was a little skeptical but figured he'd humor Pete anyway. Neither had any experience managing or owning a restaurant, except for a brief two-month spell when Dick waited tables long ago. That was the total experience for both.

The restaurant was located across the street from the Ringling School of Art and at one time George had a good business but his philandering with the young female art students pissed off his wife and that put George in a nasty divorce.

The Idle Hour Bar's owner, Inez, was the grandmotherly patron of many of the school's art students. For years she had been buying and decorating the Idle Hour bar and her home with an assortment of student art works and, because her bar was across the street, she made friends with the restaurant's troubled, absentee owner.

The restaurant had been closed for almost six months. Dick expressed his concerns as to what condition the appliances were in and how long it was going to take to get it ready to open but more importantly how much more than the purchase price would Sue's dad be willing to pay out before they made any real money to live on.

The restaurant was situated on the Tamiami Trail; the town's busy north to south highway, and in the corner of a long narrow, uninteresting, single-story Flamingo pink and blue trimmed stucco building.

Two sides of the restaurant had glass sliding doors and windows and decorated with decals of palm trees and flamingos to keep customers from walking through the glass. Besides the decals, other tenants did their best to add character to an otherwise architecturally innocuous structure, by decorating with plastic Flamingos, alligators, and monkeys.

The restaurant's twenty-foot high sign faced the busy traffic; a concrete wall with the name, "the Ringling Café," was hand painted in bright blue, lower case letters. George was no artist and too cheap to hire professionals to paint his sign.

Only two other tenants occupied the building. Sarasota's most popular gay bar and hang-out for Ringling students, The Northside Tavern. On the other end of the building, a tanning and nail salon; a favorite grooming place for the female art school models. They were good customers, flocking in to take advantage of the liberal discounts George gave them but they became the source of George's marital troubles.

Before his divorce, George had focused more on the models and not enough on the restaurant to make it profitable. His interest faded every day over his marital difficulties and dread of his soon to be ex-wife's revenge made him nervous. George began leaving the cafe for long periods of time until he finally closed the door for good.

The Idle Hour and the Northside Tavern had no food license and that gave George and the Dairy Queen, across the highway, the advantage of being the only restaurants near the school. Neither one served pizza; only toaster oven heated sandwiches. It was decided that pizza should be the main menu item because of its popularity; cheap to make, and ease of fixing; free coffee as a bonus to Ringling students. It looked like a great investment for Sue's dad.

Always happy to see them, Inez fixed Pete and Dick a pitcher of beer, pretzels and pickled eggs for breakfast before showing them her most recently acquired art treasure. She had collected so much art work that she circulated the paintings weekly from the back room to the barroom.

Inez had outlived two alcoholic husbands and made the Idle Hour the most popular bar on that side of town, especially with the Ringling crowd. Her first husband died after severing an artery when he walked through a glass door at George's newly opened café. To prevent the same thing from happening again George put the flamingos and palm trees on the glass doors.

Inez's second husband fell over dead on a pool table one night, gripping a cue stick in one hand and a young, attractive art school model in the other. That incident was the best free advertising that George could hope for; bringing in flocks of curious customers. Inez wisely remained single after that and dedicated her time to her art collection and the Idle Hour bar.

She said she would call George to bring the keys so they could get inside for a better look. They gulped down the last of their beer, to chase the hard boiled eggs, and walked across the street.

Outside, at the restaurant's entrance alcove, were three old but working penny pin ball machines that local kids played after school. Peering through the unclean, smeared glass they saw two dust-covered pool tables, a jukebox, several booths and stained Formica eating bar flanked by blue, worn plastic covered, mushroom like padded stools mounted on chrome stems.

The electricity had been turned off but there was just enough sunlight, filtering through the windows that they could see the place was in desperate need of cleaning. Pete looked a little dismayed and lost for words but was excited enough to insist that this was looking like a good deal anyway; and besides, it wasn't his money.

George, Sue, and Sue's dad, showed up about the same time. George, living in perpetual fear of his ex-wife, nervously unlocked the door and raced back to the Idle Hour to hide in case his ex was watching the place. All in all, it wasn't quite as bad as it appeared when they were outside looking in, but it did need a thorough steam cleaning and disinfecting.

The worst was a pile of grease in the corner behind the grill. Covering the putrid mess, live and dead roaches gave life to the pile of waste; something unrecognizable that pulsated in the dimly lit corner that looked like something alien that could threaten civilization. Her dad agreed it was a perfect spot for a pizza joint and after looking around, Dick agreed with Pete that the place did have potential; it was in a prime location. Surrounded by foodless bars and the Ringling School they would have plenty of customers; the bar owners also agreed that a pizza restaurant would help their businesses. That was all Frank and Sue needed to hear.

They rescued George from the back room of the Idle Hour. Frank dated and signed a very soiled and wrinkled sales agreement George had been carrying around with him for weeks, hoping for such a moment. Inez signed as witness and as Notary made the deal legal. Frank pulled an envelope, stuffed with three thousand dollars in small bills, from his shirt pocket and handed it to George. Pete and Sue now owned a restaurant.

Dick was anxious to be on his way to the islands but promised to stay for the wedding and help with the long, messy cleanup, the painting, and all the red tape involved in leases, license applications and inspections. With cash in hand, George skipped town and out of reach of his ex-wife before the day ended.

Pete and Sue inspected the equipment and furnishings. The grill, light fixtures and everything else in the restaurant, including the windows, were covered with rancid grease. The refrigerator interior was moldy but easily cleaned. The unpleasant surprise was opening the commercial size floor freezer. They assumed it would be in the same neglected condition as the refrigerator.

Pete was the first to open it and the stench, like a sledge hammer, knocked him against the stainless steel sinks. George had left behind more than forty pounds of fish, several boxes of shrimp, cartons of hamburger patties, hot dogs and other assorted meats in his rush to close the business. The warm freezer was now filled with a squirming colony of thumb-size maggots. Pete and Dick moved it outside to the parking lot until they could find someone brave enough to haul it away.

Sue's dad left a couple of days later after the wedding and finding them a small bungalow not far from the restaurant. Dick agreed to move into the small spare room where he would finally get some sleep away from their bedroom antics.

It took weeks to clean everything; floors; steam clean grills; sanitize the bathrooms and bleach on everything until they could smell nothing else. Dick was more anxious than ever to leave; to be on his way south but stayed on long enough to get the place open and running.

Before getting their occupational license Pete and Sue had to agree on a name. The restaurant clean up was nearing completion and it wouldn't be long before they could open the doors for business. Then from a dense fog of marijuana smoke, swirling around the living room, Pete came up with a name; Pizza Eaters.

He got the license and hired a painter to paint a large sign for the two story wall in front of the restaurant. But when the guy didn't show up they opened for business anyway with just a hand-painted, cardboard sign on each door.

The jukebox, pool tables and pin ball machines were replaced; four pin ball machines were left outside for school kids.

Pete and Dick went in early each day to finish up the painting and sat in the back room of the empty store next door, drank coffee and a few beers along with some pickled eggs from Inez. Once a couple of joints were smoked, inspiration followed and their artistic talents took over.

They wanted to give the restaurant an artistic look and began by covering the walls and doors with Picasso-like sketches. Dick's choice of designs for the bathroom doors would occasionally confuse the customers who couldn't tell the difference between the ladies or men's restroom; it was more entertaining than embarrassing.

Painting the restaurant walls provided hours of amusement for the visiting gay Northside Tavern neighbors who came over to watch. Dick was flattered when they suggested he paint the business sign on the two story wall out front. But neither Pete nor Dick liked heights and they did manage to cover George's old sign by taping paint rollers to the ends of broom sticks. All the marijuana and uppers in Sarasota couldn't give them courage enough to climb a ladder that high. They decided to leave the painting to the pros, who never showed up.

After a late evening while sitting on the bungalow floor, smoking joints and drinking beer, Dick found a piece of charcoal and became focused on the empty, white walls. With Pete and Sue's coaxing he began in the living room by sketching a series of figures on the walls that developed into an unbroken charcoal mural from living room, around the kitchen, the dining room and ending where he started.

It was almost daylight when Dick stopped, exhausted. Pete and Sue thought the sketches looked pretty good but the landlord disagreed and they were evicted. With a slight delay because they had to move, the day finally came for the grand opening.

Pizza Eaters was an immediate success. Pete had not applied for a caterer's license, necessary to sell and deliver food off premises, but they did a booming take-out pizza business anyway to the Idle Hour and Northside Tavern.

Pete and Dick developed a close business association with their neighbors but a special relationship with the Northside Tavern crowd; the only gay bar on that side of town. They were known as honest, dependable, and made great pizza but Pete and Dick also helped when locals tried to harass their neighbors.

The sign painters never showed up despite continued phone calls and pleading. It didn't take long, however, for Pete to forget about having the sign painted and there was no need for costly advertising; they soon had more business than they could handle.

The pizza ovens, once turned on in the morning,

were kept busy until the bars closed. In fact, the business shaped up to be more profitable than they had hoped for. Sue's dad came to visit several times and although still unsure about Pete, he returned to Illinois happy that business was good and his daughter was not going to be penniless. When Frank asked about the unpainted sign Pete told him it didn't matter. Their success began as soon as they opened when the Northside Tavern and gay community re-named the restaurant, Peter's and Dick's. It was time for him to leave.

Dick was smiling remembering the restaurant; his short stay with Pete and Sue and how she later ran off with a fake FBI agent. Pete seemed doomed but his luck changed when he found bales of marijuana floating in the water near the Longboat Key beaches. What he didn't smoke he sold.

Today he felt more peaceful than he thought was possible; the Jamaican drug helped. He missed Pete and Sue but was happy to finally be in the islands, thinking about pirates he read about and discovering there may be a wreck in the island's harbor. He had returned to Virginia from Florida to see friends and family before leaving for the islands. While there he revisited the college library to find a book he had seen years before. It was still there and had several interesting and exciting references to an ancient shipwreck lying somewhere in the harbor and he made copies.

He was thinking of sailing; seeing John and Phyllis when a very soft, distant feminine voice interrupted and confused him. Although pleasant it didn't quite fit in with his daydream; made him forget where he was for a minute because he had not fully adjusted to his new surroundings; the influence of the Jamaican drug had not completely worn off. He struggled to open his eyes and was surprised to see a warm, untouched drink in his hand wrapped in a tattered, soggy napkin.

The ice had melted turning the rum and Coke into an insipid looking dirty brown. The lime lay limp and pale; floating lifeless in the murky rum and Coke that now had a rainbow colored oil like slick on its surface. He rubbed his eyes and looked up from his drink to see where the soft, inquiring voice had come from. Still not completely alert, he saw the figure of a woman standing next to his table. He didn't know what to say.

"Are you okay," She asked apologizing for startling him, but she wanted to know if there was something wrong with his drink. "Just lost track of time," he said, "guess I fell asleep and forgot it."

She suggested a fresh drink. Dick had napped holding onto his drink and his hand was now soaked with the soggy napkin disintegrating on the glass. He smiled, handed her the watery drink and dried his hand on his almost dry Levi's.

Dick admitted he knew nothing about rum so she suggested Mount Gay from Barbados; much better because Don Q often left a rainbow slick on drinks. She said nothing was wrong with the rum; just a different technique in distilling. Mount Gay would be better. He agreed to try it.

She took the glass, wiped away the pool of water, smiled, and faded into the bars darkness. She returned a few minutes later with a fresh Cuba Libre; lime on the side this time. She did advise him against drinking the cheap, locally distilled Pott Rum; made from singed molasses; delivered by barge from San Juan. She said he should avoid their, "three bottles for a dollar," specials. She lingered.

As a distraction he opened and tapped a new pack of cigarettes against his palm until one slid out, lit it, inhaled deeply then exhaled a cloud of blue smoke before taking a sip of his new drink. "Not a bad cigarette," he thought. He couldn't help but stare; trying to think of something to say.

In the dim light of the room, with the distant bar light and Wurlitzer behind her, Dick could make out a hint of gray hair that formed a glistening halo around her head atop a well shaped body. Although he saw little of her face, the thin circle of light seemed almost out of place with her dusty voice and youthful shape. Before he could unlock his mind enough to begin a conversation, she excused herself to deliver refills to another customer.

When she walked to the far end of the bar, he was struck with how attractive she was; long prematurely gray hair fell below her shoulders, gathered into a pony tail that swayed from side to side as she walked with deliberate, well rehearsed movements of a fashion model. Nervous and excited, Dick watched; finished his drink and asked her for another one.

He was attracted to her; wanted to have a conversation but didn't know where to start and struggled desperately to come up with something to say without sounding stupid before she came back. He didn't want to say anything that would be embarrassing or sound too corny. It had been a long time since he was that attracted to someone. She returned with his drink, introduced herself as she put his drink down. "I'm Jean, do you mind if I sit for a few minutes?" she whispered and before he could answer she slid into the seat next to him.

Dick was hoping she couldn't see how nervous he was and awkwardly stuttered his name as he moved to give her room. He told her he just arrived from Florida. She asked what brought him to the island. "Nothing in particular," He answered, "but I do have friends here." He thought it would be fun to tell her about Pete and Sue but changed his mind; maybe some other time. He wasn't too sure how she would take to Peters and Dicks.

As he became a little more comfortable talking with her he learned she and her husband were from New York; he owned a bar in Manhattan and she had been a model and a Breck Shampoo girl appearing on back covers of a variety of women's magazines. That, he thought, explained why she was able to walk so seductively.

He dried his hand on his pants again. In spite of the cold air conditioning a nervous trickle of sweat made its way through his beard and down to his chin. It wasn't the heat this time. It was her. He put his cigarette in the ashtray, held out a nervous hand and she held it gently and with a surprising grip. As they shook hands he couldn't help but notice how pale his hand was, compared to hers; their clasped hands looked more like a magazine ad promoting ethnic brotherhood. Dick started to sweat again and reluctantly slipped his hand slowly out of hers then lit another cigarette forgetting the one in the ashtray. How comforting smoking was, he thought; like a pacifier.

She told him that she and her husband Larry, she

pointed at the bartender, had moved to the islands two years before and after several minutes of small talk, put her hand on his thigh, squeezed gently as she excused herself to take care of some other customers. She promised to return then slowly slid out of the booth. He watched her glide away, his thigh hot where she touched him. He had been aroused watching and listening to her but now a full range of passionate thoughts quickly came to mind; his groin ached watching her drift away and across the bar room floor.

He finally noticed that she was wearing a tie died tank top embracing her ample breasts, and a loose tropical wraparound skirt that accentuated her narrow waist. As she walked it fluttered loosely, exposing shapely tanned legs; adding more fuel to active imagination. She was a beautiful woman and he just knew she had to see the hungry look in his eyes. He couldn't help it and was grateful for the near dark cover of the lounge.

Jean returned and, while standing next to the booth, she turned slightly revealing more leg, pointed again to the bartender and loudly introduced him to Dick. Awkwardly, he turned in his seat, "Hi, I'm Dick," he said waving with a slightly raised hand, and in response, "Welcome to Paradise, I'm Larry," the bartender waved, smiled then returned to mixing drinks.

Even though he knew the bartender was her husband, it became more uncomfortable now with the introductions; he felt vulnerable and slightly embarrassed not knowing for sure what she wanted. When he thought about it later he admitted to himself that perhaps he misunderstood; the hand on his thigh or the warm hand that slipped slowly away. She sat down in the same place moving uncomfortably close next to him.

It took a little time and a couple more Cuba Libres but Dick began to talk more. Trying to hide his nervousness he asked questions about life in the islands. Jean talked freely about the pros and cons of living there; high rent, food costs, the weather, and Dick asked about sailing, jobs and dating.

Jean said they owned another bar and restaurant in the Sub Base, where she usually worked, but because their regular girl was ill she was working the airport bar. She gave him an open invitation to visit her at the restaurant.

It was getting late. He said he had to leave, finished the last of his drink on his way out, put the glass on the bar and tried unsuccessfully to avoid staring at Jean's firm nipples poking like little elfin noses from under her tie died top, or stare at the seductive thigh high slit in her skirt. "What would be revealed," he thought, "if it were a bit higher.

He said goodbye to Larry, shook his hand while Jean, holding his other hand, coaxed him gently out of the bar, through the gift shop and into the brightly lit, busy airport lobby. He squinted as his eyes stung and watered at the sudden brightness.

She pulled him gently to her, cupped his cheek in her free hand and gave him an unforgettably, full kiss, pulled away then another kiss on the cheek like she was putting her signature on an invitation; a period after a delightful sentence. She made him promise to visit her at the restaurant; he agreed before she turned, waved then disappeared into the bar. He was coaxed into a waiting taxi. He looked back to get another look at her but she was gone. They would meet again.

A New Face In Paradise

Plunge boldly into the thick of life, and seize it where you will, it is always interesting.

Johann Wolfgang Von Goethe

In a fog of passion, still thinking about Jean, he didn't notice for several minutes that the taxi driver was driving on the left side of the road. Suddenly he felt a lot like he did on the plane; this cab was also a part of the total picture of his paradise; an untested adventure and with Jean's unspoken promise the heat of the tropics paled in contrast.

The taxi's radio boomed unfamiliar but delightful rhythmic, ear-splitting, steel band music. It was slow going through the crowded streets. He remembered Jean said everything and everyone on the island was like that. No rush. The pace of island living was slow whether driving in traffic, keeping appointments, doing a job, or showing up for work. But driving slow through town was important to the driver. Seeing someone he knew he would stop and have a conversation as traffic backed up or occasionally slowed to a snails pace to lean out of the window and pat a surprised young woman on her behind.

With apparent lack of interest in delivering him quickly to Yacht Haven, Dick was able to look at everything; get his bearings to familiarize himself with the town. Shiny tin and terracotta tile roofs were sprinkled like flowering trees over the green hills; its tropical lushness interrupted by pre-war concrete water catchments that looked like dried scabs covering an old wound.

The slow ride also gave him the chance to take a mental note of where the interesting waterfront bars were; Palm Passage, Trader Dan's, the Carousel Bar, Creque's Alley and Duffy's Bar surrounded by duty free shops. Places to buy cheap cigarettes ($2.50 a carton), Orange Julius for breakfast and souvenir shops for gifts to send back home. Everything was crowded together; many in ancient stone buildings with thick fortress like walls built to withstand storms. Some looked old enough to have survived the days when pirates raided the town.

Today, like many days, flocks of tourists from several cruise ships, docked on the other side of the harbor, were carelessly dashing across the road with their burdens of cameras and souvenir filled bags; some stopping long enough to snap photographs of rustic blue, white and red island schooners tied up alongside the docks selling cargo or loading merchandise to take to other islands.

Each boat was pretty much the same in design; made of hand milled timber, random planked decks and crooked masts; their crude construction giving them a deceptively un-seaworthy appearance; more than capable of withstanding the rigors of ocean travel and each with its own color scheme of blue and white, with red trim.

Oily decks were littered with fly covered de-feathered chickens, an assortment of fresh sea food, varieties of unfamiliar exotic fish including conch, removed from their shells and arranged in squirming rows of brilliant Flamingo pink; Dick thought they looked like pink tongues; their beautiful shells would be sold separately and made into melodic conch horns or for decorations.

Dick's driver stopped every hundred feet or so to talk with some one he knew or a girl he wanted to know. If not chatting up an acquaintance they were delayed by pedestrians or behind other taxi drivers doing the same thing. The whole scene was filled with shouting, horns honking, and a crush of people gave the streets and sidewalks the look of a large metropolitan city. Added to the acrid stench of stale urine and fish lingering in the afternoon tropics the smells and sounds of the waterfront seemed more like a movie set. When he could see the harbor between the crowds Dick thought that somewhere out there could be the remains of an ancient wreck; treasure.

At last, after being slowly taxied through town, his driver pointed across to the east end of the harbor to a fleet of sail boats at anchor; their masts swaying as if trying to break free of their moorings. The taxi pulled up to the Yacht Haven Hotel and marina, the driver impatiently announced their arrival, gave Dick a gold toothed grin, took his money, gave no change, and sped away to scoop up a nearby confused group of pasty, cruise-ship arrivals.

He threw his bag over his shoulder, walked through the hotel lobby, past the restaurant and swimming pool, onto the docks and walked into his new life.

FEARLESS FRED'S FRIGORIFIC FRATERNITY

Life is adventure, not predicament.

James Broughton

The sun seemed hotter than when he arrived just a few hours ago. Jean was still lingering; he could smell her subtleness but with a deep breath of refreshing, warm salt air, her aroma and the stench of the waterfront were overpowered by familiar smells of spar varnish and paint.

What looked like a forest of bare trees from town was a vast fleet of sail boats in the marina. He walked down the dock passing several boats in their slips gently rocking up and down; swaying side to side in the water's swells, their bowsprits, like scolding fingers, pointed at boats moored in the harbor; dock lines softly squealed as they gently pulled against the dock's cleats. Dick stopped to study their sleek polished shapes, bright varnished teak trim and tall, swaying masts. His heart beat with so much excitement and envy it felt to him like his chest would explode at any minute.

Then he singled out the one boat he liked; a shiny, 12 or 13 meter Chou Lee ketch but no bikini clad babe on the deck, like in the magazines. He felt closer to living his dream than he had for years.

Dick walked along the dock admiring the different yachts before he came to the only building on the pier; the nerve center of the marina; charter fleet and yacht sales. The boater's social life gathered at Fred's busy bar where a crudely painted driftwood sign, "Fearless Fred's Frigorific Fraternity," hanging lop-sided from a rusty nail over the sweaty beer cooler, announced the bar's name; known throughout the island's as just Fred's.

The bar was one of two businesses in the building but the only one without walls on two sides with a north and west exposure; a panoramic, unobstructed view of the yacht-filled marina.

It didn't take long for Dick to notice that the success of Fred's bar was due in large part to its proximity to the ladies shower; a key to the social life of the marina. There was only one difference between the men and women's shower; a sign nailed over the doors. As the first tenant, Fred decided the ladies shower would be next to his bar so he made and hung the sign without objections. Since most of Fred's customers were men they agreed that it was good to have the ladies shower next door. It kept customers moral high.

Dick pulled up a bar stool, put his Army duffel bag down and relaxed, looked around at the bar crowd and became very self conscious about how out of place he looked. His rolled up long sleeved shirt was definitely out of place as were his un-faded jeans and calf high leather boots. Mostly though it was how pale he was in contrast with everyone else at the bar who were dressed in blue jean cut-offs, faded "T" shirts, stained deck shoes or construction boots. A cold beer sounded good.

He reached into his pocket, pulled out the last of his money, paid for a beer and started a conversation with the bartender; a guy named Andy who turned out to be a crew member on the famous Brigantine Romance anchored out in the harbor. They swapped small talk about life in the islands, local women, boats, and Andy's experiences sailing on such a famous boat. Then Andy asked if Dick knew a game called liar's poker. That was Dick's opportunity to pass the time; maybe win enough cash to keep him going for a while. He was quickly drinking up what little cash he had.

Fred showed up making a rare early afternoon appearance, according to Andy, to have a cold beer and collect some of the day's receipts. He interrupted their liar's poker game long enough to introduce himself. Fred's smoking had taken its toll. Because he was unable to work the bar anymore, Fred depended on a group of part-time bartenders, mostly guys that crewed on boats, to help with his business. If one left on a trip, someone else would takeover; no full time bartenders, only stand-ins.

Fred went to the other end of the bar to talk to friends and Andy told Dick how Fred got the nick name of "Fearless Fred." It was during the return leg of a St. Croix sailboat race that Fred went up the mast to fix a jammed halyard; apparently something he shouldn't have done. When he got as far as the spreaders high above the deck, he froze in fear; unable to move, his arms and legs wrapped tightly around the mast. Fred was being whipped back and forth like bait on a fishing rod until the boat reached Yacht Haven where two of the crew went up the mast and helped Fred down. Fearless Fred was born as was Fearless Fred's Frigorific Fraternity. Embarrassed, he never sailed again but accepted future positions as a judge aboard racing committee boats.

Dick was taking unfair advantage of Andy, who was being distracted from their game of liar's poker, winning as Andy waited on customers and talking about Fred. Liar's poker was a popular bar game and would be his tap-root for ready cash and it wasn't long before Dick had most of Andy's money.

Fred returned and continued his conversation, between coughing and wheezing, telling Dick pretty much the same thing Andy told him; how he relied on several part-time bartenders then asked if he would be interested. Fred didn't care who tended bar just so someone dependable and honest was there to open and close. Free beer, he said, was part of the perks.

He would come by each day to restock the beer coolers and pick up the receipts. He said business was brisk, tips good, and there were plenty of liar poker fans. How could Dick refuse? It would be a fun part-time job. Dick was surprised to learn that Fred's bar was as popular throughout the islands as Foxy's Bar on Jost Van Dyke except Fred had a ladies shower next door.

A few more games of poker, several more beers, a couple of Mount Gay Rum and Cokes, made Dick aware of how fresh he looked; white as a new sheet. He folded and slipped his stack of dollar bill winnings into his pocket, had one more beer, went to the men's room, unfolded his Swiss Army knife and tailored his clothes. When he returned he was met with cheers, applause and free beer to celebrate his first rite of passage.

When John arrived he was surprised to see Dick because he was expected several months earlier. After a few comments about the rough edges of his emergency tailored clothes and rigorous back-slapping John shuffled him around the bar, cold Schaefers in hand, he introduced Dick to; Mike, Bob, Gene, "No problem Joe," and other regulars. Last names were seldom known; used only if there were two people with the same first name.

As an ex college football player, John's athletic frame overshadowed everyone else at the bar. His heavy beard covered most of his face making his eyes seem like an afterthought; stuffed into a furry face like a Teddy bear. John asked if he would be interested in working some construction and Dick gladly agreed. With his cash flow depending on luck with liar's poker, the timing was perfect and working at the bar would keep him close to the boats and cold drinks.

He told John about his stay in Sarasota with Pete; the reason he was late getting to St. Thomas and he told him about, "Peter and Dick's Restaurant;" how it got its name, which made John laugh hard enough that tears streamed down his face; about Sue running away, and Pete stumbling into a flotilla of marijuana bales saving him from despair and financial ruin. That news made everyone at Fred's cheer, gasp and groan with jealousy.

Those listening raised their drinks to loudly toast Pete's good fortune as the two left the bar crowd and walked down the dock to John's boat, the Pinafore. Phyllis was in the galley fixing dinner, waved and said hello and invited him to dinner. They talked about her friends in Virginia; Dick repeated the story of his stay with Pete and Sue and then had one more cold beer after a dinner of fish followed by more catching up on news. It was late and Dick was tired and anxious to get some sleep so John showed him his bunk; the only place for him on the small boat; in the storage area next to the engine.

It was early in the morning when Dick woke up in a cold sweat. Yesterday he had awakened in a soft bed in Virginia and for a few minutes was confused. Something was crawling over his face, arms and neck. At first he thought it was a dream. Choking back a scream, but not the shudders, he flicked a big bug off his face that hit the wall with a loud smack. In the islands they're called mahogany bugs, in Florida palmetto bugs, and everywhere else just plain big-ass cockroaches. These were Dick's room-mates.

After the first few sleepless nights he could almost ignore them from sheer fatigue. His job with John was physically tiring and the bugs seemed to accept his presence by allowing him a few nights of rest without crawling into his shirt or on his face. Dick decided that it was possible he had become so used to them and tired from the rigors of work, he could sleep undisturbed or they decided to ignore him when he didn't go away.

It didn't take long, working outdoors, for his cut-offs to fade, cut down boots to show signs of wear and take on the island look but more important was his pale skin was tanning making him less visible in a crowd; more like he lived there and less like a new comer. His self esteem and confidence was improving. Now, he thought, would be a good time to tell John what he found in the William and Mary Library.

TREASURE HUNT

Behold the turtle. He makes progress only when he sticks his neck out.

James B. Conant

Dick had waited for several weeks before talking to John about what he found in an old worn leather bound book at the college. Getting used to living and working in a new environment was his main interest; not rushing into treasure hunting right away. He knew John was more practical and less inclined to spend his time looking for something as vague as treasure but what the hell; he was going to bring it up anyway. John would think he was nuts; crazy, especially when he found out where Dick said it was supposed to be.

Dick reached into his bag, pulled out a folded, damp and musty paper, told John briefly about finding and making some notes from the book as he handed the paper to John to read. He carefully unfolded the paper, studying each hand written note with a brief glance. To Dick's surprise he seemed mildly interested, handed them back, got two beers out of the small fridge and suggested a walk to Fred's where they could sit and talk about it without upsetting Phyllis who would think both of them were foolish.

They spent the evening talking about the one in a million chance of ever finding treasure but it did sound like a possibility and the more they talked, they discussed how to dive in the busy harbor. They both said the whole idea was stupid; "you'd have to be nuts to swim in such a polluted, shark filled harbor," John said. But that argument only made them think it could also be an interesting challenge; an adventure. Something to do.

After a few more beers, and a joint or two, they decided, just for the fun of it, to do it anyway; make at least one short exploratory dive. The combination of drinking beer and smoking a few joints had a way of altering reality and they knew the idea would probably be a whole lot different in the morning. If nothing else talking about treasure made the conversation interesting; these were islands of pirates and treasure legends.

The next day Dick went to town to find a small book Governor Paiwonski had written, about a ship that anchored in the harbor near the 1674 Danish colonial fort. According to him, the drunken crew raided businesses, harassed helpless residents, then put the torch to the town before returning to their ship with their loot including, according to Paiwonski, a Danish military payroll.

A group of angered citizens raided the ship, captured the sleeping, drunken crew, tied them up, and then pulled them up by their necks to the ship's yard arms before setting fire to the ship. From the beach everyone cheered as they watched the burning ship hiss and spew steam into the air before disappearing into the harbor's water. The payroll, according to all accounts, was never recovered.

That was enough for Dick. Now he was excited and couldn't wait to tell John. The log book he found in Williamsburg and the governor's account seemed to confirm the existence of a ships wreck somewhere in the harbor. The trick was to find it.

Dick needed some diving gear but more importantly lots of practice; lots of training. Professional diver Gene Archie owned and operated a small dive shop at the marina. Gene said he was happy to help, took him by the elbow, pulled him outside and pointed to a swim fin above his door. A large, jagged, crescent shaped piece was missing and not two inches from where his toes had been. "A shark," Gene said, "attacked me from behind. You should go to Secret Harbor for practice." He got his point across. It was a shark free beach and a popular topless beach with the girls; a good place to swim without any really dangerous fish; just an occasional inquisitive barracuda. Octopus was also common there; fun to watch and curious, sometimes following divers.

Before giving him any diving equipment Gene took Dick to the relative safety of Morningstar Beach to teach him the necessary diving basics. Dick was a quick study and after a few afternoons with Gene he finally picked up his dive gear, and happily headed for the pleasant and relative safety of Secret Harbor.

The beach was more than he could ever have imagined; bare breasted women swimming over head and in the clear water it was difficult to keep from reaching out and touching one.

Concentrating on why he was there, Dick swam to a comfortable place to sit motionless, resting against a small coral head, just ten feet below on the sandy bottom. Swimming around him were beautiful tropical fish he had only seen in pet stores; just inches from his mask. However, it was his experiences of his first dive, watching topless girls pass overhead, that taught him how to breathe to conserve oxygen.

Rapid, uncontrolled breathing would quickly consume the precious air supply. If so many half naked girls were able to cause him to breathe rapidly, he knew his oxygen wouldn't last very long if he came face to face with a shark so he took as much time as needed to learn how to relax.

The result was he exhausted his air supply by paying more attention on what was going on above him and not on his air supply and startled several girls when he exploded out of the water, sputtering and gasping for air.

If not working on the week ends, Dick was sitting under the clear blue water at Secret Harbor, teaching himself, with a little guidance from Gene, to dive at different depths; swimming to get accustomed to the bulky equipment, swim fins, play with the fish and an inquisitive red octopus, and all the time thinking about diving in the harbor inspired by the thoughts of discovering treasure.

Gene thought it would do Dick some good to get some experience of real diving; suggesting a dive on a popular shallow wreck on the west end of the island. Dick didn't expect it to be as pleasant as Secret Harbor but he was a little nervous but game. The wreck was an old, rusting WWII coastal freighter; now covered with thick, colorful growth and populated by a wide variety of fish.

After a short ride on Dave Beauchard's dive boat, Dick fell in behind a small group of Gene's dive students, floated for a few minutes to get used to looking down at a wreck t hat seemed so far away.

Most of the hatch covers had been blown open as the ship sank making it easy to explore the passages and rooms below; home to an exciting array of underwater wildlife; a place Dick didn't want to go. He felt more vulnerable down here away from the delights of Secret Harbor so he stayed uneasily exploring the outside of the ship with Gene who stayed close by.

On the main deck Dick discovered the deck house and while looking for a way in found a partially open, rusty iron door. It wouldn't budge and the opening was too narrow to squeeze in even without air tanks. He swam over to one of the portholes and peered into the dim cabin. Broken china, rotted metal tables, rusted chairs, broken light fixtures, covered in fans of sea life swaying in the currents, and thick rust colored silt covered the cabin floor.

Then a gigantic fish unexpectedly swam past the porthole obscuring what little light penetrated the cabin's interior. Stunned by the sudden appearance of what he thought was a shark, Dick's reaction made his hair bristle on the back of his neck and he almost spit out his mouthpiece. When he finally calmed down and his heart returned to normal, he slowly approached the port hole and looked again into the cabin. Whatever was in there, it was big.

He looked cautiously around the cabin and on the

other side saw a massive fish the size of a refrigerator; remains of rusting spears dangling from his huge body. He couldn't count them all but he thought there must have been at least a dozen. The big fish seemed to ignore them as he swam lazily from one end of the cabin to the other, his huge mouth, large enough to engulf a man, slowly opened and closed.

He swam lazily, following Dick from one port hole to the next as he swam around the cabin. The fish was brushing against the walls as if trying to dislodge the rusty spears. He had no way out and Dick had no way in.

Gene said the huge fish had become a pet with divers who named him Grover; deciding it had been confined to the ships cabin from the time he was small enough to swim through the portholes.

With limitless number of fish swimming in and out of the cabin his appetite was more than satisfied and with no reason to leave he grew until he was unable to get out. Divers, who had not been on the wreck before, had impatiently speared him only to discover there was no way of getting the trophy size fish out.

Grover would no sooner overcome his injuries before he was shot again and again. Finally the word got out that he was a pet of Gene's and other divers. Grover had become a legend; protected by friendly divers who would show him to new comers and students. The word among his growing number of fans was, "don't mess with Grover."

Before John and Dick were to make their dive, Dick went to rent his dive gear. Gene told him that when he was diving on the ship with a group of his student divers they failed to see the old curious grouper, when they first got to the wreck.

Gene said he tapped on the cabin sides but the old fish didn't come so he swam to other port holes and finally saw Grover lying on the cabin floor, mouth rapidly opening and closing, gasping his last breath, a shiny new spear protruding from his head.

Apparently someone, who had not been to the wreck before, didn't know it was not possible to remove the giant fish. Sadly Gene and his divers stayed there and waited, like friends on a death watch, until Grover died. Then, Gene said, almost choking up, a school of hungry Barracuda, circling nearby, descended on the now lifeless fish.

The day of the big dive finally arrived. It had taken several weeks of concentrated effort but Dick steeled for the inevitable dive away from the safety of Secret Harbor and Gene's watchful eye. He and John finished a small construction project and headed for Fred's. "I'm about as ready as I'll ever be," Dick said, "and if I meet anything bigger than me, I'll be the first one out of the water," he whined and John laughed.

They borrowed a small boat from dock master Bob Smith, loaded their equipment and headed to the other end of the harbor for a test dive to check the waters visibility. During those first brief dives they looked to see if there were any telltale signs of shipwrecks. A couple of coral encrusted cannons, rusted remains of two amphibious, convertible rental cars, covered in mud and green seaweed, several cheap, unreliable, English seagull outboard motors commonly thrown overboard by unhappy owners and other trash littered the bottom; discarded by passing boats. Visibility was good enough. Because the islands untreated sewerage was dumped into the harbor there was a thick brownish streak in the water they avoided.

On the morning they decided to begin a serious search, they spotted a large dredging barge that had slipped into the harbor overnight. Curious they went to Fred's to see if anyone had information about what was going on with the barge. It happened that Fred was there to stock up the beer cooler and told them it was deepening the turn around lane for the larger cruise ships and taking the sand to a cove near the sub base to build the Wayne Aspinall high school.

The dredging barge changed their plans but if careful it was possible they might be able to use the barge to their advantage.

Dick and John returned to the Pinafore, unrolled charts of the harbor, and plotted where they thought the barge was located. They decided to dive as near the barge as possible without arousing the operator's suspicion. They had nothing to lose and, maybe with a little luck, the barge would unknowingly siphon off enough sand to un-cover some evidence; a long shot but just maybe uncover the shipwreck.

They got their equipment together and went over to the barge. Being cautious John hailed the operator and got permission to tie up to the barge.

"We were hired by an insurance company," Dick told him, "for a local car rental company that lost several rental amphibious cars in the harbor. We'd be willing to help spot your suction hoses if allowed to use the barge to dive from."

Following a lot of curious small talk about the islands,

jobs, where the women were, and the islands nightlife, he gave them the okay.

At first the water was cloudy from the dredging but eventually they got their bearings and were able to see by swimming upstream from the suction hoses. It wasn't long before John, who was near one of the I-beam anchors, motioned to Dick he found something. Pushed to the surface of the sandy bottom John spotted what looked like a pile of blackened, soggy wood. They carefully moved the wood, brushed away some sand to reveal several blackened coins fused together and two thumb-nail sized gold coins. Their one in a million chances seemed to have paid off.

The scattered pile of rotten wood looked like a ship's remains and nearby several coral encrusted cannons lay in the bottom of a shallow hole where the sand had been sucked up by the barge. Several curious but harmless reef sharks were swimming nearby but Dick was too excited to let them be a bother. His rapid breathing was the result of finding the coins; not the shark.

With the discovery they needed to find out more about the wreck. How to get more information about the ship, without letting anyone know about the discovery, was a problem.

They moved the suction hose to another spot away from the wreck to avoid losing any artifacts or treasure. With air supply getting low they returned to the barge. John kept the coins gripped tightly in his hand. It was difficult hiding the excitement from the dredging operator; explaining they would be back the next day.

After removing their diving gear and untied the boat, they hurried back to Yacht Haven and Fred's for a cold beer. During the short boat ride back John said little; minds busy thinking about the discovery they had just made. Now the hard part; figuring out what to do next.

After explaining what they had been up to they gave the coins to a surprised Phyllis to clean. She was less agitated with John for running off with Dick on some hairbrained scheme once she saw the coins.

Maybe the dates and mint marks would reveal more information about the ship. The gold coins were well worn, foreign maybe French but told nothing about the wreck. It was a long restless night, with little sleep.

The next morning, a stop at Fred's for a cold beer. Maybe a plan to recover more coins would magically come to mind but then they saw the barge was gone. The water was calm making it ideal for diving but without the barge diving would be riskier; more noticeable.

After some thought they decided check out the spot where they had been diving anyway. They dropped the anchor, swam circles above the dredged hole and saw that it was quite a bit larger and emptier than the day before. Only the cannons remained among a few scattered pieces of the ship's remains.

They decided to go where the barge was unloading the sand; find out what was going on before they panicked. They got into the boat and raced as fast as the 25 horse power Johnson outboard motor could push them.

Once through the reef at French Town there was the empty barge just leaving. Instead of returning to the harbor it was heading west towards Puerto Rico.

They sped towards the barge to ask if he was returning; they may be in danger of losing their treasure if he doesn't return. As they passed the pile of wet sand they saw a group of children jumping, digging, and shouting. Forgetting the barge they steered towards the cove, beached the boat, and, climbed the mound of loose sand. The kids were running around, yelling and picking up gold and silver coins.

Back in the dinghy, they put it in gear and limped slowly back to Fearless Fred's for another cold beer. The treasure would be buried again, out of reach for good, but this time under the Wayne Aspinall High School.

HASSEL ISLAND

Only those who will risk going too far can possibly find out how far one can go.

T. S. Eliot

The island's character had changed dramatically since the Danish Government claimed it in 1670 erecting Fort Christian four years later. Centuries of pirate raids, slave rebellions, hurricanes and an earthquake or two, destroyed many of the island's colonial stone buildings. A few sturdy relics like the old fort, were not yet covered with thick paint, sheet rock, fake siding, cheap additions, or razed to make way for new construction; managing to make it through the centuries nearly unscathed.

Mountain roads, an industrial park, housing developments, shopping centers, and new businesses, were in the planning stage that would permanently change the colonial character of the island. Cliff-side condo developments were also in the plan. But paradise would be safe for a couple of more decades before those projects started.

Between working and sailing with friends Dick was

looking for landmarks, as he traveled around the islands that looked like a place where someone would hide valuables. With the many caves around the islands, it was impossible for him not to think that treasure would be hidden in one of those places given the history of the Caribbean.

On days when Dick had nothing else to do, he would be at Fred's bar with friends, a cold beer, talking about sailing, or just good old bar conversation while admiring the ladies going to and from the showers.

On the west side of the harbor's entrance, Hassel Island also had a fort built to protect the seaport from pirates and war time enemies. As he sailed past the island, Dick became curious about the forts remains. A couple of walls and pile of red bricks was all that was left and he became obsessed with an idea that it was a likely place to find treasure.

At one time a heavy protective iron chain stretched across the narrow harbor entrance; to be raised when necessary to keep unfriendly ships from entering the harbor. What little was left of the iron rings looked like empty eye sockets with tears of rust staining the fort's stone walls.

On a hot day in August, after several hours of sitting at Fred's, drinking cold Heinekens, Dick was convinced there had to be hidden treasure somewhere on Hassel Island and he was going to be the one to find it. If the old fort had a cistern it certainly would be a logical place to search; maybe a place no one else would have considered. Water filled cisterns seemed to be a likely place where people would toss their valuables for safe keeping; something done by people under siege during the Civil War in the states. This was the day Dick decided to explore the fort.

He grabbed a cold beer, jumped into a small fiberglass dinghy and aimed for the island. As he neared the island in a spray of salt water he spotted an uneven, weather beaten sun-bleached dock below the old fort and steered his pitching boat to its frail wooden ladder.

Maneuvering the boat with a beer in one hand, the boat's controls in the other, Dick never considered the difficulty of docking. He would do it no matter how rough the water or how shaky the dock because he was exploring with high expectations, lots of beer, and confident that the afternoon would end with a spectacular discovery.

Dick missed the dock several times before getting close enough to put a now warm Heineken safely on the pier to free his hand for the difficult task of tying to the dock; like trying to put the brass ring back on its hook while riding a merry go round, he thought.

With both hands now free he made several more passes before getting the looped end of the boat's bow line over a rusty cleat just as the waves pushed him away from the dock. With a jerk the boat reached the end of the line. The front of the boat was now the only place where he could stand close enough to jump onto the dock. Dick was able to pull the boat close enough so he could get one foot on the dock's ladder and one hand on a piling.

To pass the time, when sailing and on watch, he would count the waves to prove what someone told him; that every seventh wave was larger and now he discovered, for the most part, it was true. Today he forgot to count and the seventh wave caught him off guard.

Dick quickly grabbed the dock with both hands just as the ladder gave way under his weight. He now had one foot in the water and the other one in the boat. The next wave caused the boat to suddenly lurch further away from the dock and now he was standing waist deep in the choppy water.

Before leaving Fred's Dick debated putting on shoes before leaving. Going barefoot was something he did around Yacht Haven but that day he put on his new Top Sider deck shoes; a good decision as it turned out.

The water was crystal clear and Dick could see the crunching under his feet was a large colony of black sea urchins. He was now more than anxious to get out of the water deciding it would be safer just to wade the few yards to shore than try to climb onto the not so safe dock. After several near disastrous slips on the rocks, falling back and stepping into more sea urchins, he managed to finally drag himself onto dry land. The afternoon at Fred's had not yet completely worn off making for a difficult and embarrassing beachhead.

He struggled up the hill to the fort's pile of rubble, deck shoes squishing as he went, then removed his T shirt, and hung it over one of the fort's empty windows to dry before sitting down. From where he stood he could see the shiny green Heineken beer bottle left behind on the piling in the rush to get out of the water. Oh well, he thought, it would be there for the return trip.

Old orange bricks were scattered over the hill. In several piles, near two partially damaged walls, the building looked more like a bombed city from war movies. A stone terrace overlooked the ocean at the south end of the ruins and a few pieces of rusted iron chains remained that may have been used to hold the fort's cannons in place. The combination of the afternoon heat, the beer and watching the motion of the water below began to have an uncomfortable affect on him almost like mild seasickness so he stood up, walked over to a low wall facing the harbors entrance and with deep breaths inhaled the oceans salty air.

Dick imagined tall ships sailing to and from the island and fierce battles with pirates that must have taken place just a few yards from where he stood. He was hypnotized by the blue water, sea breezes and his romantic images of life in the Caribbean. As he looked over the ocean he thought there must be ship wrecks out there to explore but that would have to wait. For now there was the cistern—a lot less water to dive in and no bad fish.

Dick was feeling very clever; convinced that he was the only guy who thought about exploring a cistern; a place he hoped to discover valuables that had been shrewdly hidden for years.

The cistern was a brick, domed, structure that collected and stored rain water next to the ruins. He hoped someone centuries ago threw or accidentally dropped something valuable into the well and he was going to find it.

The sun bleached and warped wooden door's rusted hinges creaked as he forced it open. Below, the water was crystal clear; shapes of silt-covered objects littered the bottom. Anxiously he squeezed through the small opening and dropped into the chilly water being careful not to cloud the water by stirring up the undisturbed silt.

The shock of the cool water had an immediate sobering affect; made him realize what he had just done; jumped inside a partially water filled cistern; the door a small opening in the arched ceiling above. Floating on his back he stared up at the small doorway. Dick took a moment to think about his rather awkward situation.

Despite the apparent danger, the thought of how ridiculous he must look, if anyone saw him, made him smile. If anyone happened along and peered into the cistern they would be shocked and maybe amused to see him floating on his back, saying, and somewhat embarrassed, that he was looking for treasure.

Eventually, after overcoming his sense of doing something stupid, he decided, since he was in the cistern anyway, with no immediate plan to leave, might as well do what he set out to do; look for treasure.

Dick took a deep breath, sank to the bottom and carefully brushed away the years of silt from the largest object he could find and removed an old bottle that immediately broke on the terrace outside when he gently tossed it through the open door.

Finding several blackened coins of different sizes, he excitedly shoved them into his pocket. He had stirred up too much silt to see clearly and now the thought of escape finally occurred to him.

Standing on his tip-toes, the water was just over his chin and the door three feet above his head. Getting through the door became more important than treasure. He could always come back later better prepared; maybe bring a ladder next time but now he realized he could die for a broken bottle and a few coins.

Dick took a deep breath, squatted on the bottom and

lunged upward. After several unsuccessful tries, he managed to grab the door sill with slippery finger tips, walk up the side of the brick wall, threw one leg out and pulled himself through the door. Exhausted he lay on the warm brick terrace to dry out, catch his breath; thankful to have escaped. It would have been easier to date the bottle, had it not broken. He collected the treasured bottle pieces and tossed them into the ocean.

He got to the boat, picked up the really hot beer, took a couple of sips, started the engine, threw the green bottle overboard, and watched it sink leaving a trail of foam behind. Dick arrived back at Fred's bar, ordered a cold beer and drank away his fear and disappointment.

But he had the coins and handed them to Fred who gently cleaned them with a sponge soaked in Ajax he kept behind the bar. He handed them back to Dick; all somewhat used but now very shiny silver coins revealing the highly anticipated dates and a treasure he almost died for; three quarters, two dimes, six nickels and two silver half dollars; enough for a few more drinks. Dick didn't give up drinking but he did give up cistern diving.

A View From Above

Love begins with an image; lust with a sensation.

Mason Cooley

"There comes Julie," Jim whispered, "She has a towel and looks like she's headed for the showers." Dick looked down and sure enough not only was Julie headed in their direction, her sister Fern was close behind. This was their lucky day. Julie and her sister were very blonde, shapely Miami models on assignment for Don Q Rum; staying on the schooner, Lorraine. As they neared the showers Dick and Jim's excitement was more than they could bear.

Interest over watching the ladies going to the showers began several weeks ago. John and Phyllis left the islands for Spain for several months leaving Dick with little work. He moved from the Pinafore's engine room to Shoreline Marine where he helped friends move boats around and do other small jobs. It may have been only a storage shed made of plywood sheets but it was Dick's new home; out of the Pinafore's engine room it was a roomy 12 feet by 8 feet and furnished with a single cotton mattress on a plywood sheet supported by cinder blocks; a hose through the window for running water, an electrical cord with a bulb and extension cords for a two-burner hot plate and small refrigerator made up the kitchen. The bathroom and shower located in the marina building was shared with friends Marty and Tap so timing was everything. Dick found that living on a boat where space was limited was very much like the shed; there was no space left over for anything unnecessary. He was comfortable and with a view of Water Island, sailing yachts passing by, wild birds and a few donkeys to keep him company, life was very good; occasionally visiting Jean at her Sub-Base restaurant when not at Yacht Haven.

One day Bob Smith, the marina's harbor master, asked Dick if he would be interested in building a restaurant on the roof and behind his office. Of course Dick said he would but would have to ask his friend Jim if he would be willing to help. Bob outlined what he had in mind as Dick followed him to the buildings flat roof behind the office. Bob pointed to where things should be; how the interior should look. The design was quite simple. Afterwards Dick went to Fred's for a beer and wait for Jim.

Soon after Jim's arrival on St. Thomas, Dick first met him while tending bar for Fred. Jim's boyish freckles and tanned looks didn't seem to fit what Dick thought a former bodyguard to Frank Sinatra's notorious Rat Pack should look like. Jim said the pressure was too much so he quit, flew to Miami, bought a thirty-foot trimaran, sailed to St. Thomas, stopping along the way in the Bahamas Islands, and decided to stay at Yacht Haven for a while.

Dick went to find Jim and tell him of Bob's planned

restaurant. He spotted him sitting alone at the Yacht Haven Hotel's outdoor bar in deep thought. Dick ordered a beer and sat down to discuss Bob's project.

"Hey, man what's up?" Dick asked and without a word Jim pushed several official looking, water stained papers over to him.

"Read this shit," he said. "

It was a letter from a sizeable population of lawyers in Arizona informing him that a major oil company was interested purchasing land he owned next to a planned highway interchange.

"I only paid twenty five hundred bucks for that pile of desert sand and they want to turn it into an oasis for trucks."

"So what's your problem?'

"They've offered $350,000, that's the problem." He turned back to his scotch, tossed it down and ordered another one.

"I wished I had a problem like that," Dick joked.

"Well, problem is my ex-wife owns half and already gotten more outa' me than she deserves. That bitch," he half whispered over his glass, "I don't care what it costs, I'll figure out a way she and her boyfriend won't get any more," then he fell silent.

Jim told Dick that she had run off with a black jack dealer from the casino where he worked. He could see Jim was getting pretty worked up, so he just nodded, handed him back the letter and finished his beer but not before mentioning that Bob Smith asked about building a restaurant. Jim turned and nodded; not wanting to discuss it at that moment so Dick decided to go back to Fred's.

Drawing the plans would be easy. Dick's experience drafting residential plans would prove to be an asset for sketching the very simple design of the restaurant. Because he enjoyed drawing on napkins for the soft, almost artistic, effect of ink lines, he used the unending supply of Fred's handy bar napkins for the rough drawings.

Fred's became Dick's unofficial office where he could relax and drink. A growing stack of napkins attested to the endless ideas that came to mind on how to transform a simple structure into something interesting. Another joint; another beer and it became the Taj Mahal.

The one story building was a perfect rectangle; simple, boring architectural palette of weathered white painted wood siding; almost as interesting as a flat roofed military barracks. Situated in the center of the main dock and fuel pier, with a network of concrete docks that radiated at right angles, it was the busy hub of activity that supported a fleet of yachts and was the marina's social life; an ideal spot for Fred's bar and Bob's upstairs restaurant.

From his very small second-floor office, Bob could over see and manage the comings and goings of all the boats, dock activities and, when completed, his restaurant.

Dick gathered up his stack of limp napkin drawings from the bar, some of them blurred by spilled beer, and moved to a table in the sun to let them dry. Jim finally showed up, in a better mood, studied the pile of napkins, suggested a few minor changes, like discarding the elaborate, joint inspired, artistic renderings. After the drawings dried out, they took them upstairs and laid them out on Bob's desk.

Dick didn't think Jim would be interested after discovering how much money he would come into but surprised him when he agreed to help. Bob looked on as Dick explained his ideas in detail while re-sketching the plans from napkins to a paper note pad as Bob made changes; Jim then suggested a construction schedule. Bob was impressed with the detailed sketches of the finished restaurant, the estimated time and costs.

After a brief stop for another cold beer at Fred's, they were headed for the lumber yard. Bob said it would take several weeks for the kitchen equipment to arrive from Miami, so there was plenty of time to build the roof, frame in the restaurant, and complete most of the interior.

Dick laid out the floor plan on the restaurant's floor with blue and red chalk lines so they could get a good idea how everything would fit; tables, counters, kitchen and storage cabinets. It began to take shape. Critical was where the holes for the expensive electric and plumbing would be drilled. There weren't too many choices. Bob liked the layout.

Between afternoon beer breaks, some new chalk-lines for minor changes were added; plumbing the only problem. Satisfied and confident they were doing a good job, Dick and Jim impressed Bob even more by coming up with a plan to reduce costs for the plumbing by tying into the ladies shower rather than running exposed lines to the bar.

By the end of the week, the restaurant floor had taken on the look of a large Jackson Pollock painting; hundreds of colored chalk lines crises-crossed each other. There were chalk lines everywhere, the result of smoking joints with cold beer chasers, and there were more colored lines for relocating the dishwasher, sinks, stoves and refrigerator; Bob said he was impressed that they could make sense of so many lines; explanations sometimes awkward.

Now able to concentrate on the building, with the plumbing issue solved, the corrugated pitched metal roof was the next big project; important so they could work out of the hot tropical sun and preserve the finished artistic chalk drawings from afternoon showers; critical for completing the plumbing and electric.

Once the roof was done they erected a four foot high wall to enclose the restaurant; completed the staircase; finished the built-in tables and benches and serving counter that separated the kitchen from the dining area. In the meantime Bob was frantically trying to locate the long over due restaurant equipment.

With time on their hands, waiting for the missing equipment, Bob asked Dick if he would be interested in managing the restaurant after Dick made the mistake of telling him about Peters and Dick's restaurant in Florida. He said no.

"It wouldn't be the same," he said, because a job running a restaurant here would take up too much of his time." Besides, it was something Dick didn't really want to do. It didn't fit into his definition of living in Paradise.

Days passed with no equipment in sight and Bob was getting anxious. Jim and Dick were ready to begin drilling holes and put in the plumbing. The West Indies Trading Company insisted Bob's order had been shipped from Miami; scheduled to arrive within a day or two (island time); they said he would be notified when the shipment arrived.

Another day passed and Bob stormed over to the shipping offices to demand they track his shipment. Before he could get to their offices, he discovered an uncovered pile of shiny, expensive, stainless steel restaurant equipment. It lay in a heap on the dock.

Dick's brief time on the island had taught him that island business doesn't have a sense of urgency; everything would eventually take care of itself; nothing was important enough to interfere with a good time or social pastimes. Relieved but mad Bob returned with the equipment; putting it safely upstairs in the restaurant.

Now the rooftop began to look less like a dance hall and more like a restaurant. Decisions were made to run the plumbing the shorter, and cheaper, distance into the ladies showers.

Once that was determined the chalk lines were covered up with sheets of linoleum flooring rolled out, glued down and with equipment finally delivered, installing the appliances and the sinks were the last things to do to finish up. Then a major delay.

An unplanned distraction brought the job to a near standstill. It happened when Julie and her sister, wearing very informative bikinis, were coming down the pier, towels and soap in hand headed for the showers.

Everything had gone as planned until they drilled the holes through the floor for the plumbing. Measurements had been made twice and double checked so all the pipes and water lines would be put in their proper places. Then several holes were drilled; all in perfect alignment ready for the equipment.

There are times, in life, when unexpected and wonderful things happen; some can be unforgettable. For Dick and Jim it was about to happen. As they admired their skill and precision at putting the holes in the right place, they discovered where they had drilled through the floor they had also drilled through the ceiling of the ladies showers. At the very moment they spotted Julie and her sister heading for the showers, all work stopped.

For several days sinks were shuffled from one place to another; PVC pipes were cut and re-glued, while telling Bob the delays were caused by faulty glue, wrong size pipes or they were having electrical problems; whatever it took to delay finishing the job and plugging the holes.

They took turns taking peeks at the ladies below and it gave them a rare, interesting and entertaining perspective of the female anatomy. However, despite the limitations that overhead views provided, they discovered who had natural or dyed hair color, removable body parts, implants and especially the ones who enjoyed showering together.

They watched from the unfinished restaurant as ladies approached, towels draped over their arms; clutching soaps, razors, and shampoo. Once passed Fred's they fell on hands and knees, eyes to the holes and waited.

Water cascaded over firm breasts and shapely bottoms; soap suds floated away, like a dense morning fog fading in the heat of day, revealing everything. Razors gently scraped away foam, like sleds over snow covered mountain slopes; up and down soapy legs, arm pits and cautiously around private parts then oiled leaving their bodies glistening smooth.

Then the day to finish had come; excuses for delays had to end. Dick and Jim had all but permanently damaged their eyes from sawdust, had sore knees, exhaustion from looking at so many naked women in the showers; plumbing lines were finally connected and Bob was relieved the work was at last finished. Dick and Jim agreed that meeting the ladies on their way to the showers would never be quite the same. With the restaurant open for business, Jim left for South America to trade with the Amazonian Indians and Dick waited patiently for John and Phyllis to return from Spain but Beverly would keep him occupied until they got back.

DEEP SIX

Behind every great fortune there is a crime.

Honore De Balzac

The fifty-three year old ketch, Harabel, was the first; she was old and sick. The boat was purchased by Eddy and his wife in Florida, sailed to St. Thomas to join the charter fleet, like so many other sailors, hoping to live their life in paradise. It was the same year the Mamas and Papas appeared at Duffy's in Creque's Alley, and the schooner Bird of Paradise was stolen.

Dick and Beverly had finally bought their boat and had it docked at Yacht Haven when the ketch, Harabel, sailed in late one night, pulled into a slip behind their boat and when Eddy plugged the shore power in, the skies lit up like the fourth of July. Sparks, smoke and swearing filled the marina. The Harabel had, among other issues, a serious electrical problem; the last straw for Eddy and his wife. They said that when the boat was hauled out in Puerto Rico, to be cleaned, her hull was sandblasted to remove barnacles, marine growth, and rust so it could be painted. But her hull had a weak, thin spot from years of neglect and the sandblasting opened a hole the size of a Volkswagen amidships and below the waterline. Re-plating was expensive and nearly took all their cash.

Carl, Mike, "No Problem Joe," and Dick were at Fred's when Eddy showed up next day and ordered a heavy-on-the-rum and light-on-the-coke Cuba Libre. They saw an opportunity after listening to Eddy rant and rave about the costly repairs and continued blasting the old boat. "Never shoulda' bought the son-of-a-bitch," Eddy moaned. "Goddamn boats gonna eat me alive."

Carl, sitting next to Eddy at the bar, leaned over and whispered, "You got good insurance?"

"Yeah and it's expensive, too."

"What'd happen if you left the island and your boat had an accident? Would you have a problem collecting?" Carl asked matter-of-factly.

Eddy looked at Carl puzzled. "That'd be the best thing that could ever happen." He answered cautiously. "How in hell would that happen?"

"Let's take a walk down to your boat."

Carl pulled Eddy away from the crowd, the two walked down the pier to the Harabel, and when they returned Carl introduced him to Dick, Mike and Joe. They went back to the boat to discus a plan.

"Ten grand up front and fifteen percent of the in-surance," Carl proposed; Eddy listened quietly, thought about it for a few minutes and Carl could see a glimmer of hope in Eddy's eyes that maybe he could get rid of the boat that had nearly emptied his bank account and no hopes for a charter until the boat was completely re-wired.

Eddy had insured the boat for more than it was worth; plenty more than he paid for it to cover business losses in the event of natural or man made disasters. He was definitely interested especially if a claim could be filed before the next quarterly insurance premium was due.

"And how do you plan to make her disappear?"

"Once you're off the island, the only thing you need to know is that she's gone when you get back. I have my captain's license so you hire me to take your charter. That's it. Insurance companies don't argue much if the skipper is licensed."

Eddy said he would think about it overnight but he thought it was a good plan. "I'll let you know tomorrow."

The next afternoon they met at Fred's and Eddy agreed to Carl's terms, handed over the down payment and left the island with his wife turning the boat over to Carl and Joe, Mike and Dick would be the charter party, crew and witnesses, if needed. Putting the Harabel in the history books and into the insurance company's ledger was easier than expected. Propane tanks were strategically placed against the thin hull, an ignition spark was set on a timer, the crew left on a life raft, and the boat was gone in minutes.

The Titch was next but a newer boat; a schooner built in South Africa by Arthur Holgate who successfully chartered her until it was sold; the new owner, unlike Holgate, was not successful, ran up lots of debt, could no longer maintain the boat or its hefty mortgage and was unable to sell it. Collecting insurance was his only hope. He turned to Carl, Dick, Joe and Mike for help. Dick begged out.

Sinking an old boat ready for retirement was one

thing but sinking such a beautiful schooner like the Titch was something he didn't want to be involved in. Getting the boat to sink was messy. They had to run the yacht aground onto several reefs before a hole was made large enough to make it sink.

In the months that followed other older boats met similar fates until local insurance brokers became suspicious; their companies then made it more difficult and near impossible to collect on damaged, sunk, or stolen boats without certified surveys to verify replacement costs, length of policy ownership, and only then repayment would be made on a sliding scale of current market value.

The new insurance requirements noticeably reduced the number of insurance claims and boats that disappeared but left Dick, Joe, Mike and Carl actively searching for something else to do.

Dick, Carl, Mike and Joe had always been curious about the disappearance of the schooner, Bird of Paradise that sailed in one day, quickly repainted, then mysteriously left. They learned that Beverly had an interest in the boat but she didn't speak much about it. Dick did find out the boat had appeared in several movies with John Wayne, including the movie that gave the boat her name. Beverly and her partners hoped its history would make it a popular charter boat but that was only a ruse to disguise its real purpose.

A map had been found in England that revealed the location of a cave on uninhabited Mona Island west of Puerto Rico. Supposedly it contained a vast fortune in treasure and a plan was hatched to uncover it. Building a small air strip for the government was Gene Flint who, when told of the treasure map, had a hole blasted in the protective reef to allow a landing craft bring a small bull dozer over from Puerto Rico but it failed to get close enough to excavate the hillside site. Blasting was considered but they feared the cave could collapse.

It was decided to buy the Bird of Paradise and begin a charter business to off set operating costs while serving as a cover for their treasure hunting activities on the island and a crew was hired to sail the boat to St. Thomas with Beverly on board.

But when the boat arrived in Yacht Haven, the crew mutinied, put her belongings on the dock, moved the boat to the waterfront, hastily painted the boat black, and slipped out of the harbor before help could be found to regain custody of the boat. The crew knew nothing of the proposed treasure hunt and hidden on board; the Mona Island treasure map and twenty thousand dollars, in a secret compartment.

Beverly filed an insurance claim for the missing boat but because of the rash of boat disappearances and sinking, a settlement would not be made immediately; only after all efforts to locate the missing boat were exhausted and, she was told, that could take months but the payments to her bank and insurance company had to continue. If the boat wasn't found soon she could face financial ruin.

Fortunately it wasn't long before the boat was reportedly seen in Mexico. The local authorities there were notified, the boat quickly impounded and Beverly hoped she could finally regain custody of the boat and, with Dick's help, start a charter business.

But the bank, which held the mortgage, and the insurance company, had other ideas. The boat, they told her, was to be taken to Fort Lauderdale, re-surveyed to verify its insured value and the bank insisted on auctioning the boat to dissolve the loan; now facing the possibility of added debt for something she no longer owned.

After verifying it was the Bird of Paradise, and securing the boat in Mexico, agents returned to St. Thomas and hired a crew to fly to Mexico, get the boat and deliver it to Florida. But, not far from Miami, the boat sprung a leak when a thru-hull fitting gave way and unable to stop the leak, the boat quickly sunk and the crew rescued.

The Bird of Paradise was now more than a mile under water resting on the ocean floor. When interviewed the crew left no doubt the boat was gone and without a survey to dispute the boats insured value the insurance company had to pay the claim. After being picked up by the Coast Guard they collected their delivery fees from the bank and insurance company. Carl, Mike and "No Problem"Joe returned to Yacht Haven where a grateful Beverly met them over a cold beer.

FOXY'S

Some things are better than sex, and some are worse, but there's nothing exactly like it.

W.C. Fields

Dick had not traveled to many of the neighboring islands since his arrival on St. Thomas except when Bill and he made their marijuana runs to St. Croix. But those trips were short, sometimes dangerous and fast leaving little time for sight seeing.

A weekend trip to the nearby British island of Tortola was an opportunity Dick couldn't pass up when Bill asked if he would like to go to a party at Sebastian's in Apple Bay. "It was just a short hike," Bill said, "from where we would anchor the boat in Cane Garden Bay."

The morning they left Bill pulled in for gas at the marina's fuel dock in a Boston Whaler with four native passengers including Hedley who worked at the marina. On the way to Tortola Bill said they were going to stop at the small island of Jost van Dyke so Dick could meet Foxy, have a beer at his bar and where Hedley planned to meet his girlfriend.

The island's history was long and colorful with a visit made by Columbus in 1493 during his second voyage and later named for a Dutch Privateer, Joost van Dyk who used Great Harbour for his home port. Anything pirate related interested Dick.

Although living in Tortola, Hedley found himself, "engaged," to a much older, self ordained, certified princess of Jost Van Dyke who just buried her seventh husband. Fearlessly Hedley saw an opportunity to share in the widows considerable real estate holdings, inherited from her late spouses, and have social authority over an island of fewer than six hundred.

Foxy's bar was near the island's one boat dock where shallow water made it useable only to boats like the Boston Whaler. Foxy's had not yet reached the popularity that came years later as more tourists visited the islands. It was convenient for small boats passing on their way to Tortola.

Bill turned off the Boston Whaler's outboard engine, drifted alongside the concrete dock as close to shore as possible without scraping bottom, then tied up to rusting iron cleats. The islands self proclaimed mayor, a tall black man dressed in his official greeting attire of a 50's gray striped suit complete with a wide 40's mallard duck tie, bare feet, black umbrella hooked over his arm, appeared quickly as if in waiting to ambush visitors. He was also the brother of the island princess and, according to Hedley, his future brother-in-law.

"Welcome to Jost Von Dyke," he proclaimed loudly in a deep island accent; waving his umbrella in a sweeping motion.

"Foxy open?" Bill asked tying the last dock line.

"Yeah mon. He got de coldest Heineken in de islands."

Heineken Beer was the beer of choice and served everywhere in the islands. They stepped onto the dock, each taking a turn shaking his hand, followed him down a narrow sandy path to a make shift building of palm fronds, and sun bleached drift wood furniture. "We hav' de finest bah on de island, mon." It was, in fact, the only bar on the island.

Foxy's was next to a very narrow beach maybe ten feet wide room enough for the one table made of three gray-weathered boards tied to legs of drift wood, four aluminum lawn chairs held together with frayed nylon rope, seats of wood slats, and an old church pew pulled up to a make-shift picnic table. This was more than enough seating, given the usual small number of customers dropping in each day.

The bar itself was made of an old book case turned on its side, raised up on cement blocks, and like the pew was taken from an abandoned island church. Everything else made of miscellaneous pieces of drift wood. Suspended over the pulpit, like some illuminated religious icon, hung a lone 60 watt bulb connected to the islands only generator at the grocery store some two hundred feet down the beach. The extension cords, plugged end to end, were not always reliable especially during heavy rains. Add five cents to the cost of a drink if you wanted ice (Foxy had to walk the distance for ice).

Once escorted to the bar a cold beer was offered to the mayor for his guide services. He graciously accepted and returned to his position at the dock to await the next visitor.

Not wasting much time, Hedley got a cold Heineken, mounted a nearby reluctant Canary donkey, and rode happily away to whatever marital fate awaited him with his princess. Everyone wished him good luck as he disappeared up the narrow, brush-lined trail.

Seated inside the bar were two visitors who had been stranded on the island. They were exploring and missed their cruise ship's boat that returned to pick them up. Ellis was a slightly built mustached, pale young man with a very attractive companion. Ellis introduced Julie to everyone as they pressed closer for a better view of her revealing, two-piece, crocheted bikini. It concealed little of her anatomy revealing she was indeed an all over natural brunette.

Bill offered them a ride to Tortola but they refused saying they needed to catch up with their ship which was scheduled to be in St. Thomas for a couple of days. He told them he would stop on his way back to make sure the got back okay.

Foxy brought their drinks and attention once again focused on Julie and her magical bathing suit.

During the conversation Ellis said they were from England; he was a writer of racy adult romance novels with Julie providing valuable character inspiration. They had been traveling together for several months and as he talked he was nonchalantly tweezing her nipples poking through her knitted bra with his thumb and fore-finger.

She seemed unconcerned, almost amused enough to occasionally turn slightly so he could give each one its fair turn. To show off her tan, she turned her back, dropped the bottom of her suit far enough to proudly show off her checkered rear end. The white lines on her youthful bottom formed little brown squares making her round buttocks look like a bowl of delicious Wheat Chex.

After a couple of hours of being entertained by Ellis and Julie, Bill said it was getting late and they reluctantly said goodbye to Foxy, Ellis and especially Julie.

The mayor, who had been sitting nearby with several warm Heinekens, came, as if on cue, to escort everyone back to the dock. Back in the Boston Whaler with a bag of warm Heinekens, Bill cranked the engine to life, the mayor waved goodbye shouting for them to return soon and they headed for Cane Garden Bay without Hedley.

SHEILA'S WARNING

Love is the answer, but while you are waiting for the answer, sex raises some pretty good questions.

Woody Allen

John and Phyllis finally returned from Spain and Dick had a new job teaching at Nisky Elementary Demonstration School just outside of town; assigned to the second floor, third grade remedial reading class. With no need for air conditioning in the classrooms, four large, metal jalousie windows provided an even flow of cool air into the crowded thirty-six student class room. Like all the windows in the school, there was no glass or screens so the windows remained open; a constant, fresh, easterly breeze swept through the room carrying with it the sweet tropical aromas of Frangipani tree blossoms and unfamiliar but mouth-watering odors of island cuisine drifting up from the cafeteria.

But there were other days when the winds also brought with it odors from the fleet of island fishing schooners arriving at the town's waterfront. Unable to shut the classroom windows, the pungent odors from cargos of fresh seafood would sometimes overpower the tropic aromas of flowers and the school's kitchen.

There were many pleasant moments standing at his classroom window staring at the mountains, boats sailing in and out of the harbor; daydreaming while students were quietly bent over their studies. Dick's new life in the islands was certainly turning out pretty good but teaching was certainly not his intended career. For the time being, though, it would do. The hours were good, kids were interesting, well behaved, lessons easy, and the short walk from Shoreline Marina at the sub base, where he was now living, was great.

In the classroom there were a few things that made the day more exciting than remedial reading such as learning from his students, that the United States was a group of islands connected by a series of bridges and they thought Dick's dandruff was sand in his hair (dandruff was something they had never seen). More reflective of island magical beliefs was someone by the name of the Cow-foot Woman who had invaded the island. Dick asked the kids to make sketches of her, as he had them do of many fascinating island stories, as their assignment and he kept them for many years before they were lost. Then one afternoon, after lunch, unusual things began to happen.

Dick was relaxing staring out from his favorite window enjoying the picturesque views trying to ignore the lunch time knot in his stomach, that was slowly being digested, when the odd events started. The students were quietly huddled over papers, busy scratching out answers to a short quiz. Captivated by the mountain and harbor views, it took him some time to realize just how close the school was to neighboring homes. Just under the class room window was a small, pink and green cement block home. Its red painted, corrugated, tin roof gave it a familiar look of colorful, south Miami Latino neighborhood homes.

Staring thoughtlessly at the small, square house he discovered he had an unobstructed view into its sun lit living room; close enough to see an old oriental, thread bare carpet, a well used dark green sofa with deep, worn depressions on its cushions, like birds nests, where people must have sat in comfort for many years. Spread casually, over the back of the sofa, was a faded pink flamingo and palm tree, fringed throw like ones commonly found in souvenir stores in South Florida, and scattered around the room were a few small mahogany tables; dulled from years of use.

On one wall hung a fabric hanging that looked a lot like the Virgin Mary. Good Catholics, he thought. On the coffee table lay an open pack of cigarettes next to a glass ashtray filled to overflowing with crumpled cigarette butts.

He would never have given the house any more notice except for some strange noises that began that afternoon and continued throughout the day. It sounded to Dick like short bursts from a big tire leak but only happened when he was away from the window. When he went to look at where the noise was coming from, it stopped but if he ignored it, the hissing only got louder.

The strange and mysterious noises continued each day

but, after several days of harassing noises, he was beginning to really get annoyed. Finally, one afternoon as he was walking back and forth past the window acting uninterested, he quickly turned at the first sound from the house and caught a glimpse, just before she ducked out of sight behind the window curtains, of a young girl with sun bleached, waist length blond hair. The hissing stopped for the rest of the day.

After school, when he asked, a teacher told Dick the home belonged to a widowed native French woman and her two daughters; Carol, the oldest who worked at the new Orange Julius restaurant on the waterfront and Sheila, the youngest just out of high school. It was Sheila he saw and now he was determined to find out what she was up to but he also felt a little flattered by her attention.

The noises became a daily ritual, sometimes several times in the morning and again in the afternoon. Then she became more daring; each time allowing Dick short but revealing glimpses of her. She began appearing at first in tight cut-off shorts and bikini top. She didn't need to hiss any more to get his attention. He seldom strayed too far from the window and view into the house below.

Trying not to be too conspicuous Dick would look only where he could see from the corner of his eye any slight movement from the house. When he dared to look and she knew he was looking, Sheila acted as though she didn't notice and lingered deliberately in front of the living room window. Then after minute or two, she would slowly walk away with the seductive movements of a lap dancer. It was a game of tease and Dick was more than a willing player; quickly falling in lust.

Came a day when she suddenly changed her routine. She walked slowly into the room, stood firmly in the middle of the worn Oriental rug, framed by the window like a beautiful painting, hands on her hips, feet slightly apart, wearing tight faded Levi shorts, a faded, breast revealing tank top and stared up at him with wide, unblinking green eyes. She said nothing; just stared. Dick was breathless; his pulse throbbing like thunder with joy. She then gave him a timid, waist high, quick fluttering wave of her hand, turned and disappeared into the shadows of another room. God, he thought, what a beautiful rear end.

Each day in class he waited anxiously by the window waiting for Sheila to show up but for days she didn't. Then he developed guilt feelings of the lust he had for such a young girl and the feeling didn't fade with the passing days. If anything he was miserable and tried to return to as normal a class room routine as possible; leaning on the window, staring at the boats and mountains, smelling the romantic scents of the island. His students were relieved with shorter class room assignments. More than once he glanced into the, dark, empty living room below looking for any movement; any sign of life. Nothing.

Something new in the cafeteria today, he thought. It smelled a little like fried chicken but what doesn't when it's fried. Could have been Iguana for all he cared. Sheila was gone. As it turned out, it was an island favorite; goat stew and rice. Dick got his class lined up at the door to be marched down to the open air lunch room.

Being last in line he stood waiting; looking out at the cloudless sky, and breathed deeply inhaling the smell of sweet salt air when a loud, hissing sound came from outside his window.

His class was leaving for lunch but he didn't notice. He stood alone afraid to look. When he finally got the courage to look, fearing it was someone playing a joke on him, he glanced into the home's living room and there she was; fluttering around in flimsy lingerie like a new butterfly; a fairy, glancing up at him to make sure he was watching.

As quickly as she appeared she disappeared. He hadn't noticed but lunch was over and the kids were marching back to class. From then on he was uncontrollably drawn back to the window like a fly on rotting fish; the game of tease began all over again.

On Saturdays was Dick's habit to sit at the Carousel Bar, a favorite water front restaurant and bar, visit with owners Rocky and Marie, have lunch, a couple of gin and tonics, and make week end plans with friends. The bar was also the best place in town to relax and enjoy the view of sailboats that filled the busy harbor; sometimes find a date for the weekend.

It was a particularly busy Saturday with several cruise ships crowding the harbor when Dick left Yacht Haven to help a friend move a couple of boats from Shoreline Marina to Flamingo Bay on Water Island. Finished, he went to the Carousel for a late lunch, cold beer, and his favorite pulled chicken sandwich. He almost choked on his sandwich when he spotted Sheila with her sister and mother having lunch in the back room.

He was sitting at the bar behind a large hanging stalk of bananas. She didn't see him and he was able to stare at Sheila unnoticed. Sandwich forgotten; beer got warm and his blood pressure was peaking. That was an opportunity for him to finally confront his tormentor; maybe learn why she was teasing him.

Switching from beer to drinking several island strength gin and tonics, his good sense of rational reasoning would give way to senseless wanton behavior. He thought it proper to follow island customs and introduce him self to the mother before speaking with her daughters. That should impress her. He was, after all, a trusted teacher and that should impress her; if nothing else he would get some answers from Sheila; maybe.

Dick slid off his bar stool, advanced confidently towards their table, carefully balancing his drink, and stopped next to Sheila. She was surprised to see him and blushed as he slurred an awkward introduction to her mother.

Despite the drink's numbing effects, he was determined to make a good impression. She looked at Dick suspiciously but smiled saying she remembered seeing him at the school. Being a teacher in her neighborhood school certainly had its advantages but Mom had no idea how much Dick was interested in her youngest daughter or why she had been trying to get his attention.

She introduced herself and mentioned that her husband Albert died unexpectedly the year before, leaving her to raise two daughters, Carol and Sheila, who delicately shook hands with him but when he clasped his sweaty hand around Sheila's he couldn't let go.

While gripping her hand, he mumbled how beautiful the weather was, commented about the numerous rude tourists, his teaching kids to read and other mundane subjects. Reluctantly he let Sheila slip her hand away.

Carol was the oldest, about twenty-five. Dick covered some short subjects with her, mainly about the Orange Julius Restaurant where she worked; she told him about their wonderful food, the cook from Puerto Rico, how much she liked her job and how well she did in tips; Dick yawned. He feigned interest but when she paused, he quickly turned to give his full attention to the younger Sheila. Nineteen, her mother said; the seductive object of his curiosity. Why, he thought, was she was teasing him with her near naked antics?

Eyes cast bashfully down, fluttering nervously as if embarrassed; Sheila told him they were of French descent and natives of St. Thomas; their father died last year after a shark attacked him while diving in Magens Bay. She loved the beaches especially at Secret Harbor and may have been swimming there when he was practicing for his dive into the harbor. Carol interrupted, as if to get in on the conversation, saying she was interested in the local little theatre and was planning to try out for a part in a production of, Stop the World, in St. Croix. He said, "That was great," and ordered another drink.

Dick continued with small talk but as the conversations continued he found it became more difficult to stay focused on more than the one conversation with Sheila. Carol and the mother slowly faded away as they became part of the back ground noise of the busy bar; his attention was now entirely on Sheila who was blushing at Dick's shameless attention.

Perspiration burst out over the bridge of his nose; dry mouth made it difficult to for him talk; he needed another drink. He lit another cigarette that stuck embarrassingly to his upper lip; hot ashes burned the crotch of his fingers. Those awkward moments of his revealed to Sheila, without a doubt, the certainty of his desire and in response she inched closer to press her foot against his. Like a circling, hungry hawk he was getting ready to swoop down and claim his prey. For a moment he forgot they were not alone and mom broke their moment of certain rapture by coughing loudly. The spell was shattered.

He looked at the mother, her brow folded into deep, ridges of concern that narrowed her eyes into thin, evil looking slits. She recognized the glazed, painful, unrestrained look in his bloodshot eyes. She must have seen it many times in her own youth. Now it was her baby daughter in danger.

She quickly stood, made some feeble but polite excuses, collected her girls, like a mother hen wrapping her chicks under the protective custody of her wings, and left hurriedly while her daughters were still chewing their lunches.

As they were leaving, Sheila looked over her shoulder, mouthed the word Morningstar and disappeared with mom and sister into the waterfront crowd. His system was on overload with hormones; his quickened pulse demanded another gin and tonic; fantasy swept over his thoughts like a Tsunami of desire. Monday would be another day at school and a hope to catch another glimpse of Sheila's wardrobe fashion show.

It was called Morningstar Beach because it was rumored that Herman Wouk wrote Marjorie Morningstar there and the beach is an island favorite among locals and tourists. Because of the clue that Sheila gave him at lunch, Dick went to the beach the next day with high hopes of seeing her. There were plenty of beautiful women there but no Sheila. Late in the day he left; Monday was just a few hours away.

After his disappointment at not seeing Sheila that Sunday or the next, he nearly gave in to his frustration thinking maybe he should return to Secret Harbor to enjoy the parade of topless French girls; maybe get lucky or maybe Sheila would show up there.

Several more days passed with no sightings of his beautiful antagonist at Morningstar. On the day he decided to abandon all hope of seeing her, except from his class room, he was having a drink with a group of local fishermen at the bar on the beach.

Dick started the conversation with them when he brought up the subject of how scarce good seafood was becoming; fish that were feeding near the reefs on the south side were contaminated; divers were robbing precious lobster beds causing lobster to become rare and expensive and exotic salt water aquarium fish being slurped into baggies for pet stores.

They took his observations and turned them into a conversation of how numerous barracuda are around the islands; how they only bite off just a little at a time and they were the worlds meanest, they bragged.

They watched, smiling, as Dick squirmed on his bar stool. Dick thought back to Gene Archie's shark bitten swim fin. He had made the mistake of mentioning his dislike of swimming in the ocean because of such fish and they took delight in teasing him with their conversation.

The tourist agencies, for good reason, kept shark and barracuda biting information under wraps.

Dick finally moved to another place at the bar out of ear shot and ordered another drink. He was close to being in a gin and tonic, Sheila deprived, and bored-with-fish-talk coma. He needed some new distractions before he got too drunk to take advantage of an opportunity.

Dick panned his slightly blurry vision over the beach with the hopes of someone or something interesting. As luck would have it, there were several topless young women proudly standing waist deep in the water and a few women scattered up and down the beach sunning topless on blankets.

Dick loudly mentioned to the fishermen, who had now lost interest in him, just how wonderful it was to sit with a cold drink while looking over such a bounty of topless women. That sparked something new to talk about besides fishing. They scanned the beaches, hands on their foreheads, looking at the tanned bodies around the beach making rude comments as though they had never seen topless women before. For the time being sharks and barracudas were forgotten.

This was going to be, he thought, just another day at the beach without seeing Sheila. His hopes were fading. He finished the gin and tonic, slid off his bar stool ready to leave, put on his dark Ray Ban sunglasses and looked for Sheila one more time before heading back home. He walked to the end of the bar to leave and, as if he had rubbed a Genie's lamp for one more wish, there she was.

Like a spirit she suddenly appeared standing in the water like a bare breasted Arthurian Maiden of the Lake.

She slipped in unnoticed while Dick's attention was on the conversation about carnivorous fish. The sight of her sent electric shocks into his long neglected, highly charged, testosterones that now sensitized the part which fed on those hormones like a shark feeding frenzy. He was getting out of control again.

Dick ran to the locker room, jumped out of his clothes, grabbed a pair of borrowed Levy cut-offs from his locker room attendant friend Larry, who yelled after him they had a broken zipper. He said he was in a hurry and certainly wasn't going to worry about it. He was hoping it wouldn't be noticed as he ran towards the beach taking the long way around. His humiliation was just a few feet away.

Dick jumped over a stone patio wall, onto the beach. The shock and pain was instantaneous. He had landed on the corner of an old concrete shower slab, just under the sand's surface, smashing his left heel. The damage sent shock waves traveling through his entire nervous system. Between heel and brain a violent wake of agony traveled in excruciating waves back and forth from one end of his body to the other causing his private parts to withdraw deep into his lower abdomen.

The numbing effects of his afternoon drinks were quickly swallowed up with that first agonizing thrust of pain. Beads of pain-driven sweat fired out of his scalp and forehead as he raced like his leg was broken for the relief of the cool ocean salt water. Any lusty thought of Sheila was quickly replaced by a flood of pain.

When he sputtered to the waters' surface he began to feverishly swim to get as much pressure off his heel as possible, then headed for deeper water where he hoped the buoyancy would take the pressure off his foot and relieve the pain.

He finally stopped frantically swimming and able to stand with very little weight on his injured foot, the pain eased a little. He brushed the water out of his face, pulled hair away from his eyes to see where he was and discovered with heart-arresting joy he had stopped not more than twenty feet from Sheila.

Seeing him she smiled, swam closer, stood up chest deep facing him, shook her long sun-bleached blond hair, with a quick backward jerk of her head, and pulled it away from her face.

She came closer and his pain became nothing more than just an inconvenient dull throb. The Maid of the Lake stood looking up at him with big clear bright blue eyes. Dick was speechless and began to perspire in spite of the cool water. Misery quickly gave into his overpowering preoccupation with her bare, firm young breasts; their perfection tranquilized his pain even more but then raised a new torment.

He had become so enchanted by her adolescent, self-assured attitude and obsessed with youthful breasts, he saw nothing else than her saucer like eyes when she looked up.

Dick sputtered some vague explanation of what happened as his eyes glanced between her lightly sun freckled face and fabulous youthful breasts. He continued to stare without shame as they talked about the school, laughed at the time they met in town under the watchful eye of her mother and sister, who was also topless and engaged in conversation with some guy on the diving platform.

Then, as if she suddenly became self-conscious of him staring, her eyes became downcast allowing him more time to stare. He thought perhaps he was embarrassing her or maybe she found humor in his awkward attempt to draw her into an adult conversation. With all that youthful beauty, not more than two feet from him, he stumbled over an obstacle course of a thousand words.

From the first shock of severe pain and discovering Sheila in the water, he had forgotten about the broken zipper. When he did notice, it was too late. His manly estate had risen to independence. He had no control. It now had a mind of its own.

During his painful dash to the water, and standing so close to Sheila, it found relief from its confinement by vaulting excitedly, and unnoticed through the open zipper, into the clear blue water. It would not retreat despite his attempts to put it back while trying to distract Sheila.

He couldn't help but stare and notice the interesting water dynamics between the adolescent breasts while wrestling with restoring his private parts into his shorts. Looking at her nakedness did nothing but add to his distress. He failed to retrieve and corral the errant organ so he resigned himself to let it drift about like bait hoping the cool water would calm it down.

Finally Sheila looked up at Dick, gave him a light kiss on the cheek, as a lover would do when saying goodbye, smiled, and without a word, swam ashore leaving him alone in a troubling condition. Out of the water she turned and shouted an invitation to dinner with a warning that barracuda, known to inhabit these waters, would only bite off just what they needed. That, she said, could postpone their date for a very long time.

With Sheila's warning and recalling earlier conversations at the bar, the pain swept over him again and the lusting, rigid, offending member quickly lost its' enthusiasm and hung harmlessly allowing it to be stuffed back into the shorts, safe from any hungry fish. Dick was too humiliated and in too much pain to call Sheila that night.

With help from friends, Dick managed to get back to Yacht Haven. Dive instructor, Gene Archie, was at the dock helping some people into his dive boat. Dick limped over, explained what happened, Gene brought out a crutch and adjusted it to fit. He promised to return it as soon as he could find one of his own.

Dick limped into class on Monday and noticed a brown, plainly wrapped package was waiting for him on his desk. It was a pair of Levi cut-offs, its fly sewn shut, with a note from Sheila saying they were made to be barracuda proof. She would be at Morningstar the following Sunday.

Virgin Gorda Football Authority

In the football match, everything is complicated by the presence of the other team.

Jean Paul Sartre

East of the US Virgin Islands is the small British Island of Virgin Gorda; an island with a population of maybe a thousand pleasant, friendly residents who boast of having the mysterious Baths; a popular beach made famous with its unusual rock formations, a conservative luxury Rockefeller Resort hotel in Little Dix Bay, for folks who care little about cost, and the Lord Nelson Inn for everyone else who prefer something a bit less expensive, more relaxed and not quite so stuffy.

Aside from the glorious beaches, the island's biggest asset is the friendliness and patience of its residents toward visitors. It was 1970 when Dick had the good fortune to begin a two year project with his good friend Bill Aylor; re-build the new island marinas poorly designed floating docks that were sinking. Living on the more populated and popular tourist island of St. Thomas, Dick's occasional trips away from home was to Tortola, St. Croix or St. John. But for a taste of Caribbean frontier life it was visits to Foxy's bar on Jost Van Dyke with his friend Bill Tappan. Then he discovered Virgin Gorda.

In Spanish Town, the islands only village, there were just a few buildings; a GTE utility warehouse with the island's only medical clinic whose doctor practiced on the second floor in a five room upstairs apartment, and a small outdoor bar. Patients, too ill to climb the stairs, were treated on the first floor of the crowded warehouse or at their homes. Next door a small one room post office, open at odd hours during the day, offered pick-up mail service only.

The sandy road that separated the four buildings ended at the waters edge at an unused wood dock. It had been the only place for boats to unload and load cargo for years until the construction of the new docks, now sinking. The pier's only occupant, since the construction of the new marina, was Doc John's small, seldom used weatherbeaten island built sail boat.

The roads were dusty and narrow except for a paved section abutting a national park overlooking a spectacular lobster rich tropical cove. The park and its mile or so of paved road was paid for, and donated to the government, by the Rockefeller's to demonstrate, the newspapers reported, their gratitude for being allowed to build a resort hotel at Little Dix Bay.

For tiny Virgin Gorda, only a handful of senior officials were needed to administer over the small island. There was life time resident Mr. Flax who was descended from flax plantation slaves and who served as mayor, judge, immigration officer, and building inspector.

Near town and the marina was the Lord Nelson Inn, a small, quaint hotel where Bill and Dick made their home while working on the island. It was owned and managed by Tony Mack, British citizen and talented Italian gourmet chef. Tony had the signature chef's girth and a very distinct, well groomed, thick black beard with parenthetical gray streaks on each side of his chin. Tony's fame, as a talented chef, had spread throughout the Caribbean offering him enviable opportunities to travel for well paid lectures and work shops from Jamaica to Trinidad. It was during one of his stops at the Hotel 1829 on St. Thomas that Bill and Dick first met Tony during a cooking workshop with the hotel's manager and chef, Gerhardt Hoffman. When they told him of plans working on Virgin Gorda he insisted they stay at his Lord Nelson Hotel.

Dick's first trip was a Monday morning flight to make arrangements for delivery of their equipment and get permits while Bill finished up a small insulation job at a dairy on St. Croix. As was the case on all islands his Florida driver's license was accepted only on St. Thomas. Tony did warn him that he was required to have a Virgin Gorda license; good only for the time he was working there. Permanent licenses were issued in Tortola but only to residents.

After checking into the Lord Nelson Dick walked the short distance to the bright pink, Spanish Town police station. After Joseph introduced himself they shook hands. Dick sat on a metal folding chair next to a frequently painted government gray metal desk. Joseph removed a pad of yellowed forms from his desk then carefully copied what personal information he needed from Dick's Florida license. His printing was exceptionally neat, thoughtfully executed in formal, block letters, and when finished he handed it to Dick for his signature, advising him to press hard because it was in triplicate.

He signed on the line above his signature and slid it across the desk to Joseph who opened the top drawer and removed an ancient round rubber stamp mounted on the end of a mahogany, carved handle that looked like a ship's belaying pin, removed rubber bands holding a metal lid on the ink pad, and then rocked the stamp back and forth over a nearly dry, red ink pad. With a blow, like a blacksmith beating on an anvil, he hammered its' image onto the new drivers license with a force that startled Dick and rattled the old metal desk. He blew over the ink, carefully tore it off the pad, and then presented it with a flourish, like a trophy. Carefully he folded the blue and beige cash receipt, now an official government document, put it in his pocket and paid the one dollar fee. Joseph thanked him, welcomed him to the island, shook his hand, and wished Dick safe driving before escorting him to the door. Although legal on Virgin Gorda it was good for a chuckle or two in the states.

Besides the licensing ritual, he found somewhat amusing, it was the simple act of an uncomplicated informality that revealed the true nature of the islands; a simplistic way of life that gave the islands their charm and peacefulness.

At the hotel each morning, once the peacocks, chickens and goats were chased out of the hotel's open restaurant, Dick's day began with Tony's spectacular Lord Nelson Inn, island style, breakfast. Two, two-minute poached eggs, toasted homemade bread, an assortment of English chutney, plenty of coffee and a promise that lunch and dinner, because there was no menu, would be a special surprise.

Lunch would be prepared to individual taste by either Tony or Sophia, the resident native cook. But it was Monday night's dinner, he would discover, that was a very unusual occasion.

Aside from his fine cuisine, Tony was also the owner of the islands only black and white television set. Like a god on a pedestal it was proudly displayed in the small hotel lobby, just off the restaurant and bar, under an eight by ten, gilded framed portrait of Lord Nelson. Smaller islands, like Virgin Gorda or Jost van Dyke, television sets would remain a rare commodity; not be seen by many residents for a few more years.

The island's only TV programming was popular reruns. There was no way of receiving live broadcasts from the states and programming consisted of a few late afternoon Tom and Jerry cartoons for kids, network outdated productions, and most recently after a short visit by Charles Revson, some unrehearsed, live makeup fashion shows for the modern woman.

There was limited island news, weather and sports for dinner time viewing. When the transmitters were working, TV could be viewed between four or five in the afternoon to nine or ten at night; sometimes later on weekend nights. Except for Mondays, with reruns of Monday night football games, TV was fairly unpredictable. This was the daily menu contributing to six or so hours of very random

TV entertainment. Television was not a very popular pastime.

Tony had taken an interest, after a buying trip to St. Thomas, in Monday night football. It was a recent program addition to local television but he knew nothing of the game. Then Barbara, a young lady visiting Virgin Gorda who was staying at the Lord Nelson Hotel, told Tony she also enjoyed football. After a day or two she moved her things in his apartment and tutored him.

Soon after she left the island, Monday nights in the small lobby of the Lord Nelson Inn became a crowded arena for football mania. Tony's newly acquired interest for football rubbed off on his neighbors as did his passion for friendly wagering.

Being a small island of limited resources, where everyone was family or friend, Tony conceived of an interesting, entertaining strategy for harmless wagering on the outcome of Monday night football. He proposed betting would be limited to a dinner as the grand prize for the winners. If he won, the loser(s) would supply the main course of lobster, fish or steak for the next Monday night football dinner but he would supply everything else. This was more than fair with no one arguing about the wagers since they would be invited to the dinner anyway. If he lost, Tony agreed to also furnish the first rounds of drinks; but he never lost.

On his return trip, to continue working on the sinking docks, Dick had arrived late on Monday afternoon. He renewed his one dollar cash receipt license, and went to the hotel where he found Tony entertaining a small group of dinner guests. When he saw Dick he shouted for him to join them but because of a late lunch he declined.

It was Tony's Monday night, football dinner. Instead, not sharing in Tony's interest in football, Dick preferred to watch a dart game among friends in hopes he would be asked to join in. He sat the bar, ordered a Mount Gay Cuba Libre, listened to BBC broadcast crackling news over a short wave radio; more for background noise and atmosphere, and joked with his friends at the dart board.

"Mad Dog" Fairchild, Doc John and Phil Weddick, friends made during earlier visits to the island, were in a brisk dart game. After friendly prodding and jokes, he returned to his drink to finish reading the last two pages of the St. Thomas weekly newspaper.

The big news was a young mother, who had been accused of killing her baby, was released from jail when it was determined the child died at childbirth. Out of shame and fear, she tried to hide the baby's body behind the town's water well. The event drew unwelcome attention to the island and she was charged with a lesser crime, released and returned home. Had she been guilty of murder, it would have been the first serious crime on Virgin Gorda in more than four hundred years.

The Sports column was on the back page above the brief obituary and small crossword puzzle. Dick finished the puzzle, before the dart game ended, downed the last of his drink when Tony came over, after dinner, and invited him to watch Monday Night Football with the weekly sporting crowd.

Dick got a folding chair from several stacked along the wall, found a place in the rear of the small room, opened it , sat down with his newspaper folded under his arm

and listened as everyone was placing bets with Tony—
Redskins and Green Bay Packers scheduled to play. Green
Bay was favored and attention was on Tony. He sat for a
moment, ran his fingers through his whiskered chin, and
narrowed his eyes as he studied the TV while the teams
were running onto the field. He leaned back, and announced he was betting on a Redskins victory. Not to be
left out Dick agreed with Tony and not only bet on the
Redskins, he agreed to buy drinks for everyone if he lost.

Everyone who had been watching Monday night
football with Tony for several Mondays, were good na-
turedly complaining to Dick of Tony's good fortune but
now all agreed with jeers, laughter, and good-natured boos
that he and Dick would lose; the Redskins were not favored to win. Even the announcer said, "The Green Bay
Packers were a superior team." More laughter.

Hours of back and forth touch-downs, penalties,
yellow flags, crowds roaring, cheerleaders jumping and
shouting, made the Monday Night Football crowd anxious and their guffaws filled the small waiting room as the
score tied and played into overtime. With nerves on edge
and the Redskins with the ball, they fell silent. Then, with
loud groans, foot stomping, boos and hisses, the Redskins
managed, in the last few seconds of the game, to make a
field goal winning by a narrow margin of two points.

Everyone was amazed. "How was it," they asked, "that
Tony was so lucky?" Pressed to reveal his secret, Tony just
shrugged his shoulders, "Italians just don't lose."

The beaten fans shuffled out of the TV room: some to
the bar and others home. All promised to return the following Monday with something to eat. Dick returned to

the bar getting into a dart game challenge with Mad Dog and Phil. In passing he handed the paper back to Tony with a wink; the sports page headlined the Monday night football game, "Redskins defeat Packers with last minute field goal."

However, it wasn't long before Mr. Flax, one of the Virgin Gorda Football Authority, got a copy of the St. Thomas Friday paper from Tom Resnick, All Island Air Taxi's pilot. On a return visit, Dick laughed at Mr. Flax's hand painted sign above the TV and Lord Nelson's portrait, now draped in a black banner; "Home of the Virgin Gorda Football Authority."

Here Come The Judge

Between men and women there is no friendship possible. There is passion, enmity, worship, love, but no friendship.

Oscar Wilde

Homer had been divorced from his first wife for several years and lived with his newest wife Julie aboard their catamaran, Hotei. They kept their boat near the Coast Guard dock and in front of the old fort, where he and Julie operated a small day charter business. Each day they would take small groups of tourists on half day sailing trips to nearby St. John. Their charter business was very successful and was the envy of other charter boats. They worked hard and were devoted to their business.

Without fail, the first day of each month, Homer took his court awarded child support and alimony payments (Judge Michael's insisted on cash) to the judge's secretary. For a year everything seemed to be going along well. The charter business became so profitable that reservations had them booked for six months ahead. One day Homer was shocked by a certified letter from his ex-wife's attorney.

'You are in contempt of court for non payment of court ordered child support and alimony payments. Failure to pay in full within ten days of receipt of this letter will result in further court action', began the letter. It seemed his court ordered payments had not been received for more than a year. Homer could face serious jail time in a cold, stone cell of the 300 year old fort.

Letter and receipts in hand Homer raced to the judge's office to confront the clerk of court. Calm, in the face of an irate Homer, the clerk waited until he stopped yelling and explained,

"De judge hav a shortage in de office budget." She said. "Not to worry mon," she exclaimed, "de judge know 'bout dis; no jail for you, mon."

Homer was speechless as she went on to explain that Judge Michaels approved the use of Homer's child support and alimony money to make up for the lack of office funds. She promised a check would be mailed before the end of the week.

In disbelief Homer returned to his boat and prepared Julie for a worst outcome. Following a very nervous week he returned to the clerk's office to check on the status of his misappropriated support money. The clerk smiled and handed him a copy of an official U.S. Virgin Islands government certified check for the full amount, a postal receipt showing it had been mailed by certified mail and handed him a letter of apology from the judge.

Relieved, Homer went about his charter business continuing monthly cash payments to Judge Michael's clerk a little more nervous that his money could be used to support the judge's office budget. That was the same month Julie woke up to find a great white shark had taken up residence under their boat. As Homer said, "Trouble comes in pairs."

Red Wine, a Wave, Farewell

Moving on, is a simple thing, what it leaves behind is hard.
Dave Mustaine

The day was quiet, the water calm, and the blue Caribbean sparkled under the low early morning sun. The reflections of boats appeared like a big floral wreath floating on the water and, in the center of the wide circle of yachts, the harbor's pilot boat bearing Peggy's casket on its' stern. On board a minister, Peggy's friends, and the boat's captain prepared to deliver the shiny, new bronze casket and Peggy, into the sea.

Peggy was married to wealthy industrialist Jim Richardson and lived on their sprawling estate above Frenchman's Bay. Peggy's best friend was Marty Siprelli, artist, potter, and drinking partner who worked with her at Tillet's silk screening studio.

When not in the studio, which was more than likely, they could be found in one of several bars they frequented; both alcoholics who encouraged each others drinking habit. Peggy turned forty seven while being treated at a

Miami rehabilitation center; Jim's last ditch effort to help her stop drinking.

As Peggy drove home each day after leaving Marty, she would often hit a boulder turning into their long driveway, with her Mustang causing damage to the driver's side front fender. Jim would import five fenders each year for her Christmas present.

As her drinking worsened and the crashes became more common, he began buying fewer and fewer fenders in the hopes she would try coming home without so much to drink but that didn't work. She got worse instead so he sent her to an exclusive rehabilitation center in Miami. When she returned home to the studio and Marty, her drinking resumed non stop.

Coming home one day after work, Bob Smith called over the marina PA system that there was a message. It was Jim. Peggy had died while drinking with Marty at Rusty's Roost; a burial at sea was being planned. Apparently her condition was worse than anyone thought. She had been out of treatment just a few weeks before she died.

Dick noticed Jim was unusually calm for someone who just lost his wife but thought it may have been caused by his own habit of drinking lots of red wine or, more likely, he felt her end was inevitable and was resigned to the eventual outcome.

The boats gently rose and fell silently on long, rolling, ocean swells. The only sounds came from loose ropes and rigging that slapped against wood and metal as the boats swayed from side to side. Short wisps of a breeze slightly ruffled the water's surface and no one but the minister spoke; heard by no one except those standing nearby.

Anecdotes were shared while waiting for the casket to slide into the water; how Peggy drove her Mustang convertible around the islands narrow, twisting roads at high speeds from her house to her studio.

The studio began as Peggy's idea; a place where she could devote time for creative work. Jim encouraged it hoping she would concentrate on being creative rather than spend time at one of her favorite bars with Marty but creativity never quite made it past the alcohol. Lucrative pottery contracts with Rock Resorts and souvenir shops lost or neglected.

Jim's favorite pastime was looking through his brass telescope at yachts passing his estate. Getting a haircut, a weekly newspaper, and stopping for a beer at the Grand Hotel was his only weekly outing on Fridays.

In spite of being wealthy with money to do anything or go anywhere, Peggy was bored; bored with Jim and her life on the island. He had become a recluse; seldom doing anything more than going about his weekly routine so he could return to watch passing boats. Peggy had the unfortunate freedom to do pretty much as she wanted. Visiting the town's bars seemed to fill her desperate social needs.

Now at forty seven she lay at peace on the deck of the pilot boat. Dick looked away from Peggy's casket to her house on the hill above Frenchman's Bay. Jim was not on the boat next to her casket. Everyone knew he was watching the sad events through his telescope.

Then the silence was broken by the hydraulic lifts humming to life under the casket. The platform tilted, the bronze casket slowly slid off its resting place, then gently into the water and the ocean quickly swallowed Peggy in a blanket of deep blue Caribbean. The water smoothed over the ripples and bubbles leaving no clues on its glassy surface of a burial.

The Pilot boats engines finally broke into the heavy silence, escorted a long somber procession of yachts back to the harbor, the pilot boat returned to its dock and Dick and Beverly went to Fred's bar to continue their remembrances of Peggy with other friends.

For years Dick imagined Jim turning away from his telescope after watching the last boat disappear from his view and into the harbor. He would refill his wine glass and quietly toast a farewell to Peggy. That would be like Jim because he seldom left home except on Fridays.

THE COW FOOT WOMAN

Sanity brings pain but madness is a vile thing.

Euripidies

It was very late at night when Dick sailed into a small cove
not far from the Yacht Haven Marina. Because of where
he anchored it would be necessary for him to get the boat
towed into a slip the next day and get the engine repaired.
He couldn't sleep so he sat in the cockpit with a late cup of
re-heated coffee watching the boats gently sway on their
moorings in the moonless harbor. It was finally peaceful
and while considering what he should do tomorrow about
getting the engine fixed, he thought about teaching at Nisky; how it compared to schools in the states. It was very
different and as much a learning experience for him as it
was for the kids. As was the custom in the islands, most of
his students lived with their grandmothers while mothers
worked to support the household.

Dick delighted in their descriptions of home life,
family customs, music and folk tales. As a matter of curiosity and cultural interest he often asked them to illustrate

some of the more interesting island folk stories for him. His favorite was a map of the United States they drew; illustrated as fifty separate islands.

Recently he learned of a new one that got his interest; the Cow Foot Woman. A recent arrival she had become an overnight celebrity that brought terror to the island's native residents. Family's feared for their children's safety, waiting in the school yard after school to hustle them safely home like brooding hens.

Dick never thought of Voodoo, Obeah or Black Magic as having a strong presence in the islands except for Jamaica where it was highly publicized. He had no idea what black magic was all about but saw its effects on the island residents and school kids with the arrival of the Cow Foot Woman.

Dick was fully relaxed, almost asleep, coffee gone cold when a loud squeal of brakes, screech of tires, and the sound of metal and breaking glass crashing against the concrete sea wall startled him out of his stupor. He dropped his coffee cup, stood and turned to see a terrified man running from a cab dangling precariously over the seawall, screaming that the Cow foot woman got him before being swallowed up in the darkness; echoes of his terrified screams slowly faded away. His passenger got out of the cab and began yelling; waving a disfigured hand in the air while shouting unintelligible words of rage as she chased after him.

The next day he heard it was the mysterious Cow Foot Woman; her real name unknown. Dick was told that her husband was a prisoner in the St. Croix prison where a fellow inmate, since released from jail, killed him during a fight. She was determined to find her husbands murderer using witchcraft and intimidation for clues.

With a cow's hoof strapped on her left hand she began her search and became known as the Cow Foot Woman; word of her mission spread ahead of the weekly newspaper.

After the incident with the cab driver, Dick noticed her name had been painted on stop signs, buildings, and sidewalks alongside red crucifixes and other symbols; all designed to frighten someone into revealing her husbands killer. Then she disappeared as suddenly as she arrived leaving behind relieved but nervous citizens.

THE RUSTY STONE

You are never too old to set another goal or to dream a new dream.

C.S. Lewis

Dick thought all his past treasure hunting failures would have curbed any desire to continue but every so often something would come up that gave him an idea where treasure could be found and that would get him excited again; gold was just around the next bush, rock, or hole in the ground. He no longer considered cisterns. There were plenty of other places to look.

During his free time from working Dick would go to Virgin Gorda and the beaches at the Baths; named for the huge curious boulders that clutter the beach. Virgin Gorda has plenty of unusual land marks to cause any treasure hunter to think the island as a good place to hide treasure but most especially the strange boulder strewn beach.

Some, Dick noticed, had unusual tub-sized depressions in their tops that held deep pools of rainwater and, he was told, a valuable source of scarce, fresh water, for passing ships and local residents.

He spent hours and days crawling between the boulders searching for some cryptic mark, a symbol scratched in a stone or sign that would provide a clue to treasure. Each day he explored everything about the big rocks, running his fingers over their cold granite skin, as though he could coax it to talk; reveal its hidden secrets. Each massive stone had become like an old, silent friend.

It was time for him to return to St. Croix, where he had been working, and his search of the big stones ended until the next time. Maybe there was no treasure hidden among the boulders; nothing more than another Island fable. But one large stone had an unusual rust colored stain that streaked down its side but he didn't have time, before his plane left, to look into its top. He returned to the Lord Nelson Inn to pack for the trip back to St. Thomas.

He walked down to Spanish Town to say goodbye to Doc John before leaving who had just returned from Tortola where he testified that a baby found near his office was a new born that died at birth.

Doc asked if Dick had time to help pull his small boat out of the water and onto the beach so he could caulk and paint the bottom. He couldn't remember the last time he scraped or painted the small boat but its bottom was covered in sea growth and needed to be careened to scrape its hull and smoke out the wood eating toredo worms.

Careening is a method that's been used for centuries to paint a boats bottom when there's no way of hauling it out of the water. The water at the Spanish Town dock was too shallow to get the boat close enough to careen at low tide. Doc decided to tow it as far onto the beach as possible and borrowed a bull dozer from a road crew.

They waded out to the boat, looped a rope several times around its hull near the waterline, tied just under the bow sprit and the other end tied to the dozer's blade. Doc was as excited as a kid with a new toy and after a few minutes of trying his hand at operating the big dozer, slowly backed away from the beach until the line tightened.

The boat began to slowly inch forward as he gave the caterpillar more throttle; its keel buried into the sand and stopped.

The nylon rope squealed in protest, black diesel smoke erupted out of the dozer's exhaust stack, Doc gave more throttle, the boat inched forward then began to slowly lean as planned; exposing a bottom that looked like a Chinese hanging garden.

For the moment, any thought of how he planned to get it to lean over onto its other side was lost in the success of the moment. The boat was too far out of the water, beached beyond where high tide could re-float it. That didn't matter anyway.

The old wood boat let out a loud painful groan, visibly shuddered, as in a death rattle, then collapsed under its own weight. Doc had waited too long to haul her out and the worms had feasted undisturbed on its wooden hull. The boat looked like a beached flounder.

With a shrug Doc had the boat's remains dismantled, gave the worm eaten wood to neighbors for firewood, and saved the mast, which he erected in front of his office, for a flag pole.

Mr. Flax, the island's immigration and customs officer

showed up; watched as the old boat fell apart giving helpful but too late advice. Seeing their frustration he offered to buy Doc and Dick a beer.

Across the street was the only bar in Spanish Town; brightly painted blue, open air and just opened with a new owner. After struggling with Doc's boat a cold beer sounded pretty good but after listening to the new comer from New York rant and rave, apparently trying to raise racial issues that weren't Virgin Gorda problems, Mr. Flax left and returned a few minutes later with the island's two policemen.

Mr. Flax apologized to Doc and Dick before leaving with the three men who escorted the loudly protesting man to his motel room then helped him pack his bags, took him to the airport under guard, and put him on the next plane to St. Thomas. Mr. Flax returned apologized for allowing such a man on the island but he knew nothing about the Black Panther movement except he didn't want it on his island.

Dick finished his beer, said good bye to Doc, returned to the hotel, ordered a beer and sat with Tony waiting for a cab. He was deeply disturbed over the afternoon's confrontation. He sensed unpleasant changes were coming to the islands.

The cab took him down the sandy road to the small island airport where Mr. Flax was waiting; dressed in a very official, freshly pressed uniform he tipped his official, military, dark blue hat wishing him a safe trip and apologizing again for the events at the bar. He checked Dick's bags thoroughly, before allowing him to board the plane. Then he waved, shouted good bye as he boarded the All

Island Air Taxi.

Leaving Virgin Gorda this time he had disturbing and unsettled feelings from the Black Panther experience. For the time being he managed to put aside any misgivings about the island's future hoping it was an isolated incident and think about where the next job would be.

His pilot was Tom. He shared Dick's somewhat diminished enthusiasm for treasure hunting often flying low over the islands, hoping to spot the remains of a sunken ship, a suspicious outline in the water or some unusual land anomaly not visible from the ground.

Dick asked him to fly over the Baths before heading home. He told him about the odd rust stain on one of the stones and maybe he could get a different perspective from the air. By plane the beach was just a minute away. As the plane lifted off he could see the top of the largest stone in the distance. As they passed Dick commented how different they looked from the air. Now looking at them from above each appeared more mysterious than before. Then a peculiar feature on one of the smaller boulders caught his eye. He asked Tom to turn the plane around and fly over them again. What had been unnoticed before could now be seen from this completely different angle.

The granite boulder he wanted to see had a large water-filled depression in its top. Unlike the others, the water was a deep rusty brown with V-shaped rust colored stain from the lip of the hole downward, almost to the beach. Was it caused by an ancient rusting iron chest, he wondered or simply a natural stain in the stone? One day he may finish the story.

Gold, Guns and Jail

We are not creatures of circumstance; we are creators of circumstance.

Benjamin Disraeli

He slapped the worn gold coin on the bar making enough noise to startle everybody quietly drinking at the bar. Dick saw it was Scott, who was an acquaintance from his past, sitting at the Hotel Comanche bar in St. Croix, when Dick walked in with Bill. He hadn't seen Scott since he left St. Thomas to do some work down islands. He and Bill were there to pick up a boatload of marijuana to take to St. Thomas and were surprised to see Scott.

They shook hands, bought drinks, shared a few light stories then Scott handed the coin to Dick. Bill left to get the boat ready and meet Bishop with his share at the usual meeting place, the Stone Balloon Restaurant.

Dick rolled the coin over in his fingers jealous that Scott found treasure by accident. The coin was old with dates and origins so worn as to be illegible. Scott said there could be more; put it back into his pocket, and told him more about how he found it.

Dick met Scott at Fred's bar, in the late 60's at the Yacht Haven marina, where Scott had been living aboard an old derelict sail boat on the north dock. He had been working construction, like most of the guys he was living with and, like Dick, searched hopelessly for treasure in his spare time. But his luck, unlike Dick's, changed.

He said when he left St. Thomas to go to an island where he was hired (he wouldn't tell which island for obvious reasons) to help build a small marina and yacht basin. His job was to survey the harbor bottom and mark suitable locations for the dock's pilings. It was while using small painted floats, tied to lead weights to indicate where the structures would be placed, Scott said he made an unexpected discovery.

"I was diving near a channel marker's concrete mooring anchor," he said softly, "when I saw something shiny out of the corner of my mask. It was the edge of a silver dollar size gold coin, the one I showed you, not far from where the mooring anchor was dropped."

After a few drinks, and without revealing too many details, Scott leaned closer to Dick and whispered, "I moved the anchor each day just a little bit until it was next to mark the spot where I found the coin. Each day I'd stuff a few coins into my wetsuit," he put his hand inside his shirt Napoleon-like, "until I thought I had the last of em'; sold em in Miami, bought a boat and filled her up with a load of guns." He ordered another drink as Dick sat in wonder that Scott should be so lucky. He found a treasure too, but it was lost to a bunch of kids and a high school.

The islands of Nevis, St. Kitts and Anguilla had been

in turmoil with threats of a revolution and the potential violence could make Scott rich if he succeeded in getting the guns there.

"Gotta go," he said standing. "Good to see you again and if all goes according to plan, I'll be back. Tides just right; boats kinda' low in the water and I gotta get out a' here before it gets any later or someone gets nosey." With that he shook Dick's hand and left quickly. Bill showed up soon after with the boat, they loaded up with several bales of marijuana from the familiar abandoned Lobster House restaurant and headed back to Yacht haven.

One weekend, at the Hotel 1829, Dick was having drinks with friends when Reddinger showed up with an update on his job with the Water and Power Authority. Boring, he said, but quieter with fewer politics compared to his last job as Assistant States Attorney. He said he got a call from Scott who was jailed in Miami. No one was surprised.

He told us that Scott said he was just off the coast of St. Kitts when the island's marine patrol had apparently been told, by an undisclosed source, that he was smuggling a load of guns. He suspected it was one of the fishermen at the dock in St. Thomas who approached him about buying guns.

Before they could catch him with a boat load of illegal weapons, he scuttled the boat in deep shark infested water. He was picked up, interrogated and thrown in the local jail, but the evidence against him was out of reach for the time being. The authorities were unwilling to dive into the dangerous water to retrieve the evidence, but they kept him anyway on suspicion putting him, he said, "in a jail as old and cold as that shit-hole fort in St. Thomas."

Scott said he was released, when the police weren't able to collect the evidence to prove that he was a gun runner. He was escorted to the airport and, because they classified him as an undesirable, was put on a plane to Miami where he was met by Federal agents. It seemed that he bought guns, with his treasure money, from a known Cuban arms dealer the Feds had been keeping an eye on for several years. William said he advised Scott to plea bargain by turning on his Cuban connection, assist in a sting operation that would shut them down and, if he was freed, go into hiding for a while. That was the last Reddinger or anyone heard from Scott for months.

Sitting at Fred's one afternoon Mike told Dick he was surprised to see Scott when he showed up at Yacht Haven. Everyone thought he was a marked man for his part in disrupting the Cuban gun dealers but there he was; "on his way back," he told Mike, "to where I found the gold in hopes of finding more." Then he truly disappeared.

A ROMANTIC TRADE

The prestige of government has undoubtedly been lowered considerably by the prohibition law. For nothing is more destructive of respect for the government and the law of the land, than passing laws which cannot be enforced. It is an open secret that the dangerous increase of crime in this country is closely connected with this.

Albert Einstein

Smuggling marijuana was more a romantic trade in the sixties than a risky one. It was easier, more profitable, easier to get rid of, and a whole lot safer than running guns. It was also easy to do, and free of interference from uninformed or misinformed authorities. It was a great time to run drugs because bringing marijuana into the island had yet to reach the wholesale smuggling proportions or penalties of the eighties; therefore less likely to be enforced.

The port town of Fredriksted was where most Jamaican marijuana was delivered before it went into distribution to other islands. This is where Bill and Dick met local attorney and successful bidder, Antoine Bishop, who would help make arrangements for their pick-up in Christiansted. Because it was such a profitable industry, several local well-connected citizens like Bishop, with political or social influence, took an interest in the not so risky, "consulting," business. As a rule they helped for a percentage; do everything but handle the drugs, just pass off helpful information.

It was easy money and competition among a few attorneys was so strong it seemed like a car auction; a bidding war.

A Fredriksted waterfront local bar was the meeting place; a narrow, tin-roofed building divided into two shops, walls made of plywood and burlap, offering very little privacy. The building was typical of many beach-side bars; hastily erected with plywood and tin roofing sometimes taken from construction sites.

Migrant bars, they were sometimes called, would be in business for years until some minor politician, running for office, would demand business licenses. Within hours the bar could be dismantled and relocated after a warning call from the court house.

"The Dew Drop In;" standing room only for three or four customers. Outside a couple of randomly placed round, weathered, rusty tables with several matching rusted chairs was the one place where they could talk in relative privacy over cold beer. Tables, chairs and wind torn umbrellas were, like all bar furniture, supplied by a liquor distributor; decorated with faded green and white Heineken Beer logos.

The beer was kept cold in an ice filled cooler; popular Mount Gay Rum, cheap Pott rum, Beefeater gin, cheap scotch and Coca Cola, Fanta Orange soft drink, club soda or tonic water for mixers made up the bar's limited menu. Exotic mixed drinks never offered.

Next to the bar on the other side of the burlap and plywood wall, was a very small, unassuming, unsigned and unlit shop. The flaking pink and blue lines of paint, which at one time had been evenly painted, were the only evidence there was a business next door.

Inside shelves were filled with ancient leather working tools, bottles of assorted leather dye, scraps of leather, and the unmistakable odor of glue and shoe polish. The room was too small for anything more than the old man, his tools, boxes of shoes and sandals to be repaired; customers waited at the door. There was no electricity so he powered all his tools and equipment by pumping a foot treadle connected to a large, iron centrifugal wheel. Once he reached the necessary speed he would stop peddling, race back to stitch leather on the sewing machine; a soft buffing wheel to shine shoes; powered knives to carve out sandal or shoe soles or to grind the finishing touches on leather work before the wheel slowed down.

Tucked in the opposite corner a dull yellow plastic shower curtain hid his other trade. The leather belt, used to power the shoemaking equipment, could be switched over to power a dental drill. For the strong at heart he was also the local dentist with as much anesthesia his patient could drink at the bar next door. The worn leather arms of the dentist's chair attested to the discomfort of some of his customers.

On several visits to the bar Bill and Dick saw several patients sitting outside getting anesthetized with rum;

preparing for what had to be a not so pleasant experience. If the patient passed out there was always someone at the bar to help carry him to the chair.

Once arrangements were made with Bishop for their delivery they would wait at the Comanche Hotel for him to contact them for payment; usually around the corner at the Stone Balloon restaurant where they would exchange money for a key to either a building or truck where the drugs would be stored. Today it was the abandoned Red Lobster Steak House conveniently located on the waterfront.

Bill brought the boat around to the dock, opened the door with Bishop's key, and Dick tossed several small bales of marijuana into the boat then they headed for home to anxiously waiting customers. What was brought from St. Croix on those trips was quickly sold to friends at Yacht Haven, the Sub Base and sometimes to Foxy's at Jost Van Dyke if time allowed. Then Phillip Johnston, the new Assistant States Attorney who took office after Reddinger left, decided to get involved in, "busting," what he perceived as an international drug trade.

Phillip often went to happy hour at the Hotel 1829 not far from his office in Fort Christian. There he met Dick and told him he was new on the island, recovering from a recent explosive, divorce, promoted to the job by one of his political friends in D.C., who saw his relocation as a way of saving his legal career, and potentially expensive alimony; now out of reach of his ex, he felt safe.

After a few drinks, Phillip told him that he had been planning a significant drug bust; first one ever on the island. Wanting to make an early impression on his Justice

Department superiors in Washington, he coordinated with his counter parts in Puerto Rico to conduct an early morning raid on the boats anchored in the harbor around Yacht Haven. He invited Dick along but he declined for good reason. He made his excuses, finished his drink and left.

At Shoreline Marina, Bill was working late on an outboard engine when Dick got there and told him of his conversation with Phillip about the upcoming raid he was planning. Next day they were moving boats around planning the next trip to St. Croix when Phillip showed up with two men he introduced as agents from the Puerto Rico Department of Justice; a boat was needed for the early morning raid. Tap, Bills dad, showed Phillip and his friends several boats they could use that were fast enough for what they needed.

Tap knew Bill and Dick were smuggling marijuana but agreed, when Phillip insisted, to rent them the very fast, twin engine, OMC. After Phillip left they laughed at the contradiction; Fed's using the same boat for a drug raid used to smuggle drugs.

It was late morning when the raiding party returned the boat to Shoreline Marina. Dick's curiosity was making him anxious to find out what happened that morning. At happy hour that afternoon, Phillip said the pre-dawn attack took place without incident; taking sleeping boaters by surprise. More than a dozen boats were successfully boarded, people shaken out of their bunks, boats thoroughly searched and drugs seized. Phillip, anxious to show Dick the results of the raid, took him back to his office, opened his desk drawer and instead of showing him a stack of revealing Polaroid pictures of captured marijuana and drug smugglers, he showed him three "roaches" and several marijuana seeds; the total take for the morning raid. Total cost for a handful of leftovers? Per ounce, Bill calculated, it was probably the most expensive marijuana in the world.

Soon after the failed raid Reddinger offered Phillip an executive position with the island's Water and Power Authority. With a little coaxing Dick helped Phillip discover the relaxing benefits of marijuana. He not only became a good customer he also helped with information just as his friend Bishop did in St. Croix. Their business was safe in both ports or at least until the next States Attorney moved in.

STUFFING RITA

When a woman wants to betray her husband, her actions are almost invariably studied but they are never reasoned.

Honore' de Balzac

One hot day, while drinking at Fred's after work, it was the surprise of an old acquaintance from New York who showed up. Dick was shocked to see Ted, whom he hadn't seen in years, leaning against the bar. Ted's thinly haired and oddly shaped pink head, perched atop his short narrow Polish frame, showed the affect of years working on merchant ships; his scabby scalp peeling like it was sun burned.

"Ted, what the hell you doing here," startled he almost jumped off of the bar stool like a panicked rabbit. It had been at least seven years since Dick last saw him in New York; the last guy he expected to see on the island. Shaken by his sudden and unexpected appearance Ted stood up, nervously seized and shook his hand, grabbed a beer and urged Dick to one of the empty tables near the edge of the dock; away from the crowd.

Dick jokingly asked him if they kicked him off his ship.

"I been through a lot of grief since I last saw you in New York," looking around nervously he whispered, "and they didn't kick me off my ship, they left without me." He grinned. "It's a long story."

"So, how'd you know where to find me after all these years?" Dick was curious because friends in the States never visited because he didn't want them to.

"I was scheduled to sail for St. Croix when I ran into one of your former art students John what's-his-name and he told me."

For a brief time Dick taught at the Warwick Art College before leaving for the islands. John had dropped out of school and art classes before going on to become a successful marine engineering graduate. He had been working as chief engineer aboard a merchant ship when he ran into Ted in the Norfolk shipyards.

"Well, what's been up with you since New York," Dick asked knowing he was in for a not so simple answer. Ted, as Dick remembered never did have a simple to-the-point reply because his life was always disjointed. He tried to make up interesting stories then add boring jokes about shabby seaports.

Life at sea aboard ships traveling from country to country never seemed like it could possibly be boring or simple to Dick but the way Ted told stories made everyone want to leave the room. Dick anticipated nothing different but this time he would be surprised.

"Dick, it's Rita again and one of her ass-hole boyfriends that almost got me locked in some shit hole in

Brazil," he paused long enough to toss down most of his beer. "Locked up and the key thrown away."

This time he really got Dick's interest. It sounded like it could be a National Enquirer headliner. Dick thought he knew Rita and what she was capable of but Ted's story revealed she had a new talent. Being a merchant seaman, who was often at sea for months at a time, was something Rita didn't like after they were first married. She tried passing the time with pottery, painting, knitting and a few other traditional crafts but nothing got her interest like shopping.

It didn't take long to replace her boredom with being a bargain hunter finding a compromised peace with the money he made and several boyfriends to fill in after the stores closed. When Ted did come home she devoted herself completely to make him happy. It was a very strange and twisted relationship. Dick thought they were both nuts.

As he listened to Ted, Dick sensed a strong undertone of rejection; sadness. "I been thinkin' about leaving the ships; finding somethin' else to do close to home to keep her happy; maybe start over." Ted stopped talking long enough to order another beer.

"My ship was scheduled to drop off some construction equipment in Belem," Ted paused then groaned after a gulp of beer, "supposed to be there a few days to unload. I asked Rita if she'd like to come down, do some sight seeing, maybe save what was left of our marriage."

He admitted it sounded good but it didn't turn out quite the way he thought it would. Ted stopped long enough to gulp down the rest of his beer, belch loudly and get another one.

"I can't imagine what Rita would like about Belem." Dick said, "The whole Goddamn town smells like fish and it sure as hell isn't the most romantic spot in the world."

"Rita said she always wanted to see a place like that," he said defending the idea, "because she wanted to go on an adventure."

"Well, I think you should have smelled a rat when she said ok," Dick answered a little smugly; getting up for another beer.

"Well, I never thought about it because she seemed anxious to go there." He stopped talking for a minute as if to think about why he even thought the idea was a good one. "Come to think of it she was a bit too eager."

Dick went to get two more beers. Ted continued to tell him that Rita had checked into the Belem Hotel several days before he arrived. He found her sitting alone at the bar and told him her cousin's husband Luis, from Washington State, wanted to come along for the adventure to meet some guy he knew upriver in Manaus.

After a few more drinks and pressing to know more, Ted said she finally admitted Luis was a big drug dealer in New York she'd known for a long time and agreed to help him smuggle some pure grade cocaine. If successful it meant she could make a lot of money for her and Ted; their share in the lucrative profits when it was sold on the streets back home.

Ted said he was curious about how they planned to smuggle enough cocaine to make it profitable without getting caught but was afraid to ask. He said that thoughts of potential riches made him more interested in profits than curious about Rita's association with the big black guy with gold teeth that joined them in the hotel's dimly lit lounge.

"Rita introduces me to her friend, Luis, who tells me how they plan to get rich smuggling cocaine." He can't help but smile. "You know, Dick, believe it or not it was Rita's idea to cram as much of that shit inside her as possible and believe me," he paused long enough to lean over the table to whisper, "there's a lot of room in there. And when Luis shakes his head, saying it's second only to the Luray Caverns, that's when I became really pissed off."

Ted started to laugh as though he was getting even by revealing to Dick some very intimate details about Rita. Because Ted was convinced they'd be rich he clenched his fists and curbed his anger so he wouldn't get the shit kicked out of him by a guy who outweighed him by pounds of bulging muscle. Just one trip, they told him, with the cocaine would make more money than any of them could possibly have made in a year. Ted put his elbow on the table, waving his index finger in the air as if to emphasize the point.

"That black son-of-a-bitch," he waved his finger faster, "promised a big payoff for letting my Rita cram her assets full of cocaine."

"Sounds like a good plan to me," Dick told him almost laughing. "If I had a woman endowed like Rita I'd have tried the same thing but without a wedding ring or middle guy. I'd have probably shot the son-of-a-bitch anyway for plugging my wife."

Ted goes on not too amused at Dick, "and on top of everything, while we're drinkin' and makin' plans, my

Goddamn ship left without me and my paycheck with it, leavin' me broke. Not more than twenty buck in my pocket."

He said he was to wait at the hotel, "until they sold the goods back in New York then promised to wire my share to the hotel. And Rita," he said, "was eager to do it again if she was successful. But I hated like shit to watch her leave with that black son-of-a-bitch." Ted let out a loud burp, finished his beer then got another one and sat down quietly.

Dick could see Ted was about to work himself into a drunken, feel sorry for me, mood so he tried changing the subject by asking him how long he planned on staying.

Ted told him that he needed to be in St. Croix in the morning to catch a ship leaving Fredriksted. He finally calmed down and sounded worn out from his ordeal.

"What time's the air boat leave?" he asked.

"First flight about eight," Dick said, "but a friend and I have to go there anyway so we'll take you in the boat, if that's ok," he offered, "and it's fast. We can get there in plenty of time."

Ted started again. Forgetting he was tired he went on with his story.

"I waited in that God-damn rat hole for almost a month and a half. Six weeks of signing room checks for food and booze. Then I got this wire."

Ted's face reddened as if his blood pressure would drive the blood through the top of his head. "Maybe that last beer wasn't such a good idea."

He reached into his shirt, pulled out a sweat stained, wrinkled piece of paper and handed it to Dick. It was the wire he got from Rita. It read: Sweetheart; Caught cold; bag broke when sneezed stop stuff got wet. stop. no good, cant sell. stop. sorry honey stop Good luck stop Rita

Ted said he suspected they had, "cashed in and they spent the money. If that much cocaine had gotten into her system she'd be dead."

Dick agreed but encouraged Ted to finish his beer hoping he would relax, maybe get a good night's sleep so he could get up early for the trip to St. Croix.

"Go back to your room and relax." he said trying to calm him down. "We'll talk more in the morning."

"That's a great idea, thanks dude, boat ride sounds like fun, Seven O'clock, fuel dock, right?"

"Right. If you're not there you'll have to fly."

He and Dick walked down the dock, arms over shoulders, to the front entrance to the marina's hotel. Once he was settled in Dick called Bill and told him of the change in plans.

He said they would have a passenger but Ted was cool and wouldn't be a problem. Besides he wouldn't be there when they loaded the boat. Bill agreed.

At exactly seven in the morning, Dick got to the fuel dock and Ted was sitting on the edge of the pier with his feet dangling over the water. His red rimmed eye lids hung loosely over watery eyes, squinting tightly against the morning sun; tears streaked down his cheeks, and with thinning uncombed hair, untrimmed beard, his slept in, wrinkled clothes, he looked more like an unhappy, stoned homeless person.

They didn't have to wait long before Bill pulled up in the OMC. After making quick introductions they got in and the boat pulled away from the dock. Once they were out of the harbor Bill pushed the throttle forward as far as it would go and the twin Mercruiser engines roared to life, the wind whipped the hair around their heads, the boat rose out of the water then skimmed across the waves like a surf board.

In less than two hours they had raced across the open waters into Christiansted harbor and were sitting at the Comanche Hotel having coffee before getting Ted into a cab to Fredriksted. He quickly finished his story before Bill returned from making a phone call.

Ted told Dick he was forced to sneak out of his hotel room in the middle of the night, "before the cops got there to arrest me for not paying my bill. I got on board a small coastal freighter leaving for Trinidad just in time and then I was lucky to get another one to New York that stopped here St. Croix for a couple of days." Then quietly Ted said, "I heard Rita and that scum bag drug dealer boy friend of hers," Ted paused, looked around and whispered so no one at nearby tables could hear, "were caught in Miami. She got drunk and forgot about the cocaine, climbed into the sack with some ass-hole she met at the hotel and…. well you can guess the rest. That time she almost died."

I couldn't help but laugh. Ted got up, tossed down a shot of tequila with the rest of his cold coffee and looking a little sheepish, and said he was anxious to leave.

"I gotta' go, Dick. The ship leaves pretty soon and I hafta' register yet." Ted was smiling a little as he got into the cab. Dick watched as the cab disappeared down the narrow street, Ted waving from the cab's window.

Ted quit the merchant marines, took up with a beau-

tiful young Mexican girl he met in Florida, and lives happily with her near Guadalajara.

Ten For Twenty

Each man the architect of his own fate.

Appius Claudius

Dick had just returned from a quick trip to Jost Van Dyke and Foxy's with Bill at the Yacht Haven fuel dock, tied up to a slip next to Fred's Bar and decided to stay long enough for a beer or two before going into town.

Coming into the harbor they noticed several boats anchored there had some odd looking pieces of paper hanging from their life lines; apparently secured by clothes pins. They weren't aware of any holidays, that would have people decorating their boats, but when they got to the docks there were the same odd pieces of paper hanging on other boats.

Bill and Dick grabbed a beer at Fred's and walked down the dock to see what the decorations were about and why so many boats had them. Pieces of green fluttered in the breeze like little pieces of laundry. Puzzled they walked over to the nearest boat for a closer look and found several thousand dollars of fluttering wet twenty dollar bills skirting the boat; carefully pinned to the boats rigging.

They were amazed at the number of boats that had the bills hanging out to dry and had no idea how or why there were so many boats decorated with twenty dollar bills. Afraid to ask the boat's owners they waited until they got back to Fred's for another beer to ask why so many boats had twenty dollar bills out to dry.

"No Problem Joe," was sitting at the bar and boasting to everyone who would listen, about the quality of the counterfeit dollar bills. Joe, it seems had been selling the bills for ten dollars with discounts for bulk purchases.

His customers were trying to age the crisp currency by washing it in salt water, detergents to remove the salt, then hanging them in the sun to bleach.

They were pretty good copies and could easily pass for the real money; the source of the money was Joe's closely guarded secret. Customs and immigration authorities frequently visited the docks but none noticed, cared or thought it was perfectly normal to hang money out to dry; too obvious to be crooked.

But, as with all things that seem too good to last, someone finally noticed and Joe was yanked off the bar stool at Fred's in hand cuffs, taken to jail at Fort Christian, and would have been on his way to Federal court in Puerto Rico but for friends who bailed him out. Joe didn't let the day end before leaving for someplace down islands ahead of Judge Michael's discovery that the wrinkled twenty dollar bills seemed a little bit blurry.

Stay Away From Murder

It is easy to kill when you don't see your victim.
                                        Friedrich Dürrenmatt

Dick and Bill were finishing up a small delivery to French-man's Bay and stopped at Fred's for a cold beer; visit with friends when they ran into Jim Rawls just in from Brazil. He got rid of his boat a couple of years before, collected the insurance, and married the daughter of an industrial diamond mine owner. Jim had been one of many luckless boat owners, with a lackluster charter business. He left for California after giving the keys of his decaying boat to Carl for "accidental" disposal.

The boat failed to remain afloat after a through-hull fitting gave way while on charter; flames filled the engine room when the electric starter shorted out, and an explosion made the boat unsalvageable. Jim returned soon after, collected a sizeable insurance check from Lloyds of London and celebrated his misfortune by dragging friends from bar to bar; Rusty's Roost, the Carousel, Trader Dan's, Duffy's, Up the Sandbox and finally back to Yacht Haven;

he was spending money faster than he could open his wallet.

That's when Jim first met Cynthia. It was during a brief rest stop between bars buying a new Rolex Submariner at the Little Switzerland store. Usually reserved or conservative, but with too much to drink, Jim introduced himself and learned she was traveling with her father; owner of a large Brazilian industrial diamond mine, they were in St. Thomas negotiating with the jeweler Jim Heath had been selling to before he disappeared. A date was made to meet her at the 1829 Hotel where they were staying.

With the discovery of her father as owner of a diamond mine, and with a large amount of cash from the insurance settlement, Jim was determined to know her better. He devoted a lot of time to impressing Cynthia's father that he was financially responsible by telling him that he recently disposed of a successful charter business.

Over the next two months Jim made several visits to their home and diamond mines not far from Belem for a brief courtship. Jim convinced her father he was the man for his daughter and within a few more months they were married. Now he was back in St. Thomas.

"Dick, I gotta' ask a favor." Jim asked, "Can I see you in private for a minute?"

He followed Jim around the corner of the building where he stopped to talk away from the bar crowd.

"What's on your mind?" Dick asked.

"I got a problem with some guy in Belem." He whispered, "Who I really don't like."

"So what do you want me to do?"

"How much?"

"What do you mean how much?" he asked feigning ignorance. Dick wanted him to say it.

"How much to get rid of him, that's what I mean, Dick." Jim started to look wildly around; afraid someone was listening. "How much do you want to make sure I never see him again?"

Dick didn't think he was serious so he gave him a number he thought all respectable hit men should get paid.

"Tell you what Jim, how about ten thousand and all expenses," he said figuring a guy with a diamond mine and insurance money could afford it, "Half now and the rest when he's gone," he added almost as an after thought.

Jim looked like he had the wind knocked out of his sails.

"You gotta' be kidding," he said loud enough for everyone to hear. "That's way too much."

"Well you asked and that's my fee. Talk to Mike if you think that's too much. Maybe he'll do it for fun." Dick laughed but Jim didn't think it was all that funny.

He stormed back to the bar and Dick followed to resume his conversation with Bill. He last saw Mike leaving with Jim. Several weeks later Mike showed up when Dick was at Fred's. He sat down, ordered a beer and Dick asked, "So, how'd it go?"

"Great, but I think ole Jim's not going to be so happy." Mike was smiling so Dick knew there was a good story.

"You got rid of his problem, right? So why won't he be happy?"

"Well, it was too simple and not worth the four grand he paid me. I found out what bar the guy hung out and

gave three fishermen at the bar a hundred bucks each."
Mike stopped long enough for Dick to get another beer.

"I told them," he continued, "the Gringo at the end of
the bar was paying for their drinks and I never wanted to
see him again."

"That's it?" "That's the whole story."

"That's it," Mike answered, "Too simple and easier
than handling sharks." He drank his beer in one swallow,
belched, pointed his finger at Dick and said, "It was less
personal than pulling the trigger; easier than watching a
guy gasp his last."

Apparently the news got to Jim pretty quick because
he was in St. Thomas soon after Mike arrived and Mike
was right. Jim was upset but after ranting and raving, he
calmed down over a gin and tonic admitting he was happy
that it was over; more upset that he didn't think of it himself before paying four thousand dollars to Mike.

Salvage Rights

Would you learn the secret of the sea? Only those who brave its dangers comprehend its mystery!

Henry Wadsworth Longfellow

The Holiday House, near Shoreline Marina, was an island favorite place for dinner; usually lasting two or three hours with a parade of waiters and the chef delivering several courses to their table. It was during a late dinner with friends one night when Tap said he got a letter from Tony, someone Dick and everybody knew from Yacht Haven, who had been in the charter business and was now living in the Bahamas.

We all remembered Tony beating the odds to have survived an accident that seriously burned him when his yacht, Scimitar, exploded while he was working in the engine room.

Following months of hospitalization and rehabilitation he bought another boat. "Chartering in St. Thomas," Dick remembered Tony telling him, "had become very crowded; lots of new boats moving in almost daily and the fun was gone." After being in St. Thomas for several years, he wanted to try chartering in the Bahamas for a change.

Yacht Haven was home to one of the world's largest charter fleets and Tony felt the Turks and Caicos Islands would be a better place with less competition. He wrote Tap about his harrowing trip that nearly ended before he got there and was written almost like a short story.

Tony wrote that the weather was good the whole way and his new boat, Suddenlee, was a dream to sail; her sails could be trimmed so well you could leave the helm without an auto pilot. Tony never did like auto pilots because he felt out of touch with the boat and, besides, it was hard on batteries.

It was several days after leaving St. Thomas, when he was nearing the Turks and Caicos Islands that something really bizarre happened. Tony always said that, "everything that happens is just a matter of timing."

After Tony was released from the hospital, following his near fatal accident, he met Daryl Armstrong at Fred's bar one afternoon to discuss buying his boat.

Daryl had retired from the Merchant Marines and owned a Gardner designed ketch, the Suddenlee, built in Coos Bay. He arrived in St. Thomas with his wife but his trip from Oregon had not gone as planned and was anxious to sell his new boat. His wife left him just after they arrived and told him he could return to their Florida home as soon as he sold the boat.

Tony and Daryl struck up a quick deal over a couple of cold beers that was too good for both of them to pass up; Tony would soon be on his way to the Bahamas, Daryl back to Florida.

Little had been done to maintain or make repairs on the beautiful ketch, as Tony discovered. He had to replace most of the expensive navigational electronics, rebuild the Mercedes engine and Onan generator; dangerously corroded through hull fittings were replaced and then he added an impressive array of new safety gear. The list of replaced, new or rebuilt equipment looked more like a catalogue of marine parts; "the stack of bills," he joked, "was the size of a Michener novel.

But Tony ignored the costs and stubbornly worked on refusing to get discouraged. He remained focused on sailing the Suddenlee to his new home so he could begin his new charter business. Finally he finished oiling the teak deck, the bottom paint dried and the Suddenlee rolled down the Hassel Island dry dock tracks, slipped into the water and docked at Yacht Haven where Tap helped with the final preparations for Tony's departure.

Tony was near the Caicos Islands, when the Suddenlee hit something so hard, one morning that he was thrown against the forward bulkhead and then backwards onto the galley floor. His coffee mug was shattered into a million pieces, silverware, plates and everything that was loose in the boat was thrown on top of him; charts and navigation instruments that were on the chart table were all over the cabin floor as water gushed in from the forward cabin.

When he got top side he could see nothing in the dark. There was no moon and it was pitch black except for a few stars. Then the boat began a downward slope, bow first. She was sinking. It took Tony a minute to realize he had to abandon the Suddenlee pretty damn quick.

Tony wrote the seas were pretty calm and there were no ships in sight; he had no idea what had happened; nothing he could see that he could have run into. He activated the emergency signal, gathered up a five gallon jug of water, as much emergency stuff he could cram in his life raft including a flare gun. He watched in shock and disbelief as the Suddenlee slipped below the waves. Nothing was left except for a trail of bubbles, papers, charts and other flotsam on the water's surface.

As Tap paused in telling Tony's story more drinks were ordered, dinner finished and finally desert. The chef brought in a pot of coffee and with everyone wanting to hear more, Tap was coaxed into resuming telling what happened to Tony.

It wasn't until the sun started to come up that Tony could see what looked like a blue and rust colored shipping crate just a few hundred yards away. He managed to row over and tied his life raft to it. It was a helluva' lot larger than he expected and then realized it was a jettisoned container from a cargo ship. He forgot about the Suddenlee and thought about what to do now that he was tied up to a partially submerged shipping container, several miles from the Islands without a radio.

Tony knew that by maritime law he had the right to claim salvage on anything abandoned at sea. But making a claim of salvage not only meant he had complete ownership; he also had the responsibility for the container, including any liabilities. From the time he claimed salvage, he needed to remain tied to it until he and the container reached shore and his claim was filed. At the moment it seemed almost impossible. In rough weather containers are frequently jettisoned if a ship is in danger of capsizing but the containers can pose a hazard to navigation, as Tony just discovered.

He was worried the thing would sink while he was asleep but was more concerned about how to get it to shore and how much longer he could survive on what little water he had. All he could think about was what might be inside the container. It was possible the contents could be valuable; worth maybe enough to buy a new boat but he needed a tow to shore. Grand Turk Island was, he estimated, only a day away and, with any luck, he would be in the shipping lanes.

"You won't believe it," Tap said, "but before the day ended a coastal freighter on the way to the Islands, spotted him."

After some negotiations, they agreed to tow him into shore for a small percentage of any valuable cargo. But if the contents were damaged, or ruined, at least Tony could sell the shipping crate. The rusty container and Tony was towed to the island and the local authorities came out to follow them into port; taking pictures for the newspaper the whole time. With an excited Tony and freighter crew looking on, the container was slowly raised out of the water by a construction crane, lowered to the dock, locks cut off and his treasure spilled out onto the dock; a cargo of rusted Mexican toaster ovens and crock pots.

It cost him a lot to have the mess cleaned up and the freighter's captain and crew left empty handed. Tony was left with an empty, rusty, shipping container but was surprised to find out that selling it was easier than he expected. A drug dealer from Norman Island, covered in gold chains, showed up at his hotel, counted out more than enough money for him to buy another boat and asked if he would be interested in a charter contract.

Tony wrote Tap that his new business was doing great and sent a picture of him celebrating his birthday. Tap reached into his pocket, pulled out a picture and passed it around the table. It was Tony smiling; surrounded by young, shapely bikinied girls standing around him on board his new sailboat.

"Business," Tony wrote on the back of the picture, "is better than ever and my new friends on Norman Island keep me pretty busy."

THE REVEILLE

There's no thrill in easy sailing when the skies are clear and blue, there's no joy in merely doing things which any one can do. But there is some satisfaction that is mighty sweet to take; when you reach a destination that you never thought you'd make.

Unknown

A name was never better suited for a boat than the Reveille. She was big, noisy, lazy, sloppy, poorly designed, and ill suited for what she was intended for; a potential killer but Dick didn't see that until he was a long way from land and then it was too late.

Negotiations had just finished with the sale of their fifty foot sailing yacht, Suddenlee, when Dick heard the aluminum racing sloop Reveille was planning a return trip to her home port of Cape May in New Jersey.

He stopped to talk to Phil, the boat's captain at Fred's bar, and asked if he and Beverly could go along as a volunteer crew on the trip back to the states. Phil agreed when Dick offered to pay for all the supplies for the trip as added incentive but Dick voiced his concern about sailing into the unpredictable April weather in the Atlantic. Even with good weather the trip would not be without risk but Phil was pressed for time and needed to leave soon.

Unlike traditionally built yachts the Reveille was built of aluminum, low in the water, tall mast, and flush decks; she was built for racing. The boat was costly to maintain requiring specialized fittings and treatment to combat electrolysis. Especially vulnerable, and always of concern, were the fittings that secured the massive center board to keep the boat from tipping over. The Reveille's huge centerboard was hydraulically adjusted, as sailing conditions changed, and like everything on the boat, depended on proper maintenance to keep electrolysis in check.

Built in the 60's to compete in the Newport -Bermuda race, her design was made by feeding computerized engineering data into a bank of computers in hopes of a winning design. Her sparse interior, to reduce her weight, was uncomfortable and very noisy; ringing like an aluminum bell when ever she was struck by a wave or by loose rigging banging against her mast.

Following a disappointing and humiliating last place showing, the million dollar failure was retired from racing and sent to St. Thomas to join with the charter fleet in hopes of recovering some of her dignity and building costs; neither successfully reclaimed, despite Phil's best efforts.

Earlier, while on a charter trip to Montserrat, as if to add insult to injury, the boat heeled so far over in a sudden gust of wind, she rolled onto her side and because of its size, it took nearly an hour to haul in the water-soaked sail before the boat flipped upright. Returning to St. Thomas her stainless steel helm broke in two places.

Dick and Beverly had a successful trial sail to Christmas Cove and the new owners moved onto the Suddenlee. The couple from Canada was as excited to take possession as they were to be former owners. The timing couldn't have been better as they moved onto the Reveille the same day. Dick had enough time, before they were scheduled to leave, to familiarize him self with the boats rigging and time for everyone to know their new ship mates. Before leaving everyone gathered at Fred's for last minute farewells.

They left St. Thomas on a course that would take them east of Puerto Rico and the Bahamas Islands then a straight line for Cape May; that is if there were no serious weather problems. In the event of an emergency on board, Bermuda or one of the Bahamas islands would just be a few days away.

The first series of storms occurred only two days into their trip. During the peak of one storm an unfamiliar, frightening sound, shook the entire boat like a huge sledge hammer. Everyone rushed on deck to see it was the stainless steel forestay that had snapped with a noise that resonated throughout the aluminum hull, as if struck by another ship. Phil hurriedly turned the boat around to put the wind behind them to push the mast forward. With the strain now on the back stays, Dick took the helm while Phil rigged with the repairs by clamping a line to the broken forestay and back to a winch near the cockpit. With the line drawn tight to support the nearly one hundred foot mast, the Reveille returned to her original course. The storm lasted until late in the afternoon and to everyone's relief the repaired forestay held.

More storms came up suddenly late that night forcing another course change. As the strengthening wind shifted directions it became necessary to add a second person on watch. With the continuing bad weather and course changes, Phil was now uncertain of their position. The next morning a cargo ship was spotted coming in their direction; Phil decided to hail them and ask for a position fix but they ignored the international telex flag and the radio remained silent. He tried to call them on the radio and once again no response. It was time for creative and dramatic efforts.

Phil was concerned they were nearing dangerous waters and desperately needed to get information from the passing ship to accurately chart their location so he changed course to intercept them. Dick went forward and fired a red distress flare, and the two girls, Beverly and Phil's girlfriend Loren, dressed in bikinis, stood on the bow holding a makeshift sign with the radio frequency hastily drawn on it, hoping that some of the ships crew was looking through binoculars. It wasn't until they removed their bras that the ship came to a full stop.

The Reveille looked very small next to the towering ship and, with the topless girls flirting and waving to the crew, they were able to get close enough that Phil could shout a request for the ships LORAN coordinates. After making several passes, to the delight of the ship's crew, the information was successfully relayed and to show their gratitude Phil sailed past once more so the ship's crew could have a last look at the girls before sailing away.

With a new position plotted Phil discovered the weather had driven them so far off course that they were dangerously close to the treacherous Silver Banks. Although it would take a few days longer, Phil set in a new course for Bermuda. Everyone agreed a stop would allow for emergency repairs to the forestay and a good chance to relax after fighting so many storms. But the weather had other plans.

It was after a very stormy night that a strange and eerie silence woke everyone just before the sun came up. Hearing nights of the high pitch of wind; feeling the boat slam into high seas and being sprayed by mountains of salt water, it was strange to suddenly hear nothing and that made everyone feel a little nervous.

When Dick went on deck he found everyone staring at an ocean covered in a thick blanket of oak colored Sargasso seaweed as far as the eye could see; glistening in the hot morning sun. The Reveille was surrounded by the weed and gently rose and fell almost imperceptibly in the windless morning; limp sails, like laundry hanging up to dry, moved only slightly as the boat gently rolled.

They had been blown into the area known as, "the Sea of Dead Ships;" a place where there is no wind or current. For a sailing ship dependant on just wind power, caught in the grips of the tenacious weed, its' crew was often condemned to a painful death from starvation or lack of fresh water.

It took the Reveille two days to get out of the thick seaweed. As seaweed became twisted tightly around the propeller and shaft, the engine over heated and to relieve the strain it was necessary to remove the weed. Diving in water several miles deep made Dick very nervous but he took his turn anyway to cut the seaweed from prop and shaft. Following two days of using their drinking water to keep the engine cool, rationing their fresh water became necessary.

As the seaweed began to thin out everyone was relieved to be free of the deadly seaweed when a slight, welcomed breeze, then a gentle wind, finally filled the sails. As the day progressed they were sailing through an ocean almost free of seaweed, the winds began to increase, as did dark gray clouds, then blackening skies that promised more storms. Another course correction, as the strong winds shifted them away from their course to Bermuda, and put them on a new course for North Carolina.

Loren and Beverly informed them, after lunch, that the refrigerator's ice had melted sooner than expected and, before it could spoil, they had fixed the last of the refrigerated food. Typical of everything on the boat designed to reduce weight, the refrigerator was small with room enough for a few days of ice. With ice and all refrigerated food gone they were left with a few cases of canned goods; baked beans, plenty of spaghetti, spaghetti sauce, crackers, a few cans of V8 juice and a warm six pack of Shaffer Beer. The beer and V8 juice put in an insulated cooler on deck where any one on watch was required to change the seawater to keep it cool.

The tenth or eleventh storm - Dick had lost count - hit them just a few days off the coast of North Carolina; one storm would end, another would follow within hours. Dick was on watch when the boat suddenly heeled over putting her rail in the water. He rang the alarm bell, alerting the sleeping crew that he needed help.

He nervously rubbed his hands over the Reveille's helm where it had been repaired, expecting them to break again from the strain. He turned the boat around, now going in the opposite direction to put the seas and wind behind the boat, to ease the strain on the rigging and the repaired fore stay and Phil and crew could reef in the sails; something that seemed to be a constant activity.

Then unexpectedly Lou, one of the other passengers, appeared from below, staggered over the slippery deck to position himself behind Dick. He was in a panic and jumped on Dick's back shouting, "you're going in the wrong direction; I need to get home." Lou was trying to gain control of the helm, and with his arms around his neck, Dick lost his grip on the helm, the boat jibed, and the heavy aluminum main boom swept violently from port to starboard.

Dick ducked to avoid getting hit with the boom but Lou wasn't as lucky. He was caught in the traveler and lines behind the helm. The force of the boom knocked him overboard but before he disappeared into the angry, black water, Dick was able to grab him by his belt loop. To keep from also being pulled over the side, Dick put his leg and arm through the helm to maintain control of the boat.

Lou was screaming and dangling over the life lines, only inches from the white capped waves; Dick's grip on his belt loop the only thing that kept him from falling into the ocean. When Phil saw the trouble he was having he rushed back, grabbed Lou, pushed him down the hatch and told him to stay there.

Relieved that he was out of the way, everyone turned

their attention to the dangerously unsupported mast. With a reefed main and reduced head sails they felt it was possible to carefully jibe a second time but slowly, and return to their course, putting the supporting backstay on the correct side. To everyone's relief the forestay repair took the strain and everyone returned to their bunks. The weather finally eased for the remainder of the night, Dick gave up the watch to Phil and went below and slept soundly.

The last storm, before making port, hit them violently less than fifty miles from Moorehead City. The sails had become so wind torn they were almost useless; there was no fuel and what fresh water was left was contaminated. There was no food, and to make matters worse, in the morning light, they could see the turbulent waters of Frying Pan Shoals and its light tower through a gray mist of rain. Earlier that morning Phil had become concerned enough for everyone's safety to radio the Coast Guard for assistance. Without sails or engine the Reveille was now being relentlessly pushed by heavy seas and gale winds closer to the deadly shoals.

The seas were so high and the morning full of rain, that the mast, despite being almost a hundred feet above the deck, was invisible to the Coast Guard. As the morning wore on Phil instructed everyone on emergency preparations if they were forced aground on the Shoals. Dick frantically went to their cabin, the engine room, opened cupboards and storage areas and discovered to his amazement the Reveille had one untested, eight-man self inflating life raft, no safety harnesses, no sea anchor, and no life preservers.

When the life raft was pulled out of its container (the emergency release didn't work) it laid flat on the deck; Dick tried the inflating canister but it, too malfunctioned and efforts to inflate it with a foot pump failed because the raft was so rotted it wouldn't hold air. There were few options left so Phil raised the center board as far as he dared, lowered all but a few feet of the shredded main sail and tied the rest to the boom. The reduced sail, he hoped would be enough, to act as a wind rudder to keep the boat heading into the wind and seas.

To reduce the backward movement towards the Shoals they needed a sea anchor so Dick suggested everyone gather up their clothing and tie them into a big ball. Once done he threw it over the bow with a line fastened to a forward cleat. That, Dick hoped, would slow them down enough, giving them time needed for the Coast Guard to find them before they hit the shoals. If not the most they hoped for would be to ride the waves over the reef providing the centerboard was high enough.

Suddenly Dick spotted a small battleship gray Coast Guard boat. It appeared, disappeared and then appeared again on the crest of a large wave several hundred yards away. Each time it was seen everyone cheered; its arrival just in time. A line was fired over to the Reveille and after several lines snapped, they were finally towed safely into the seaport town of Moorehead City.

At the dock, everybody waited impatiently with the Coast Guard for the arrival of immigration and customs officials. Until then they were unable to leave the boat or dock. While waiting, they got off the boat, sat on the pier and tried to relax as they stared at the storm ravaged boat.

The Coast Guard remained to make sure everyone stayed together until cleared to leave. Dick looked over the torn sails and the damaged boat in disbelief when thinking that the boat had no life saving or emergency gear on board. When he recounted the storms they experienced, he became angered at himself for not being more diligent not noticing there was no proper safety or life saving equipment on board and at Phil for putting everyone in danger.

Dick went below to get cleaned up; something to do to help pass the time. One by one, the rest of the crew followed. After getting the boat and themselves spick and span, then gathered in the cockpit to recount their harrowing days at sea. Dick pointed at something no one had seen before while sitting on the pier. All heads turned to see a small diner at the end of the dock getting ready to open up for the day. But, no matter how much they pleaded with the Coast Guard, they wouldn't allow them to go ashore until the powers that be checked them in.

They watched as inside the small restaurant, clearly seen through its' large plate glass window, people scurrying about getting the restaurant ready to open. There was a couple of counter top plastic vats that began bubbling with iced tea and what looked like lemonade. Their stomachs audibly growled and cramped painfully at the sight. Adding more misery to their pain was the aroma of French fries, hamburgers and other cooking odors drifting in the wind and down the pier. They imagined fried fish, hot dogs, baked beans, coleslaw, sandwiches, and their mouths watered uncontrollably.

Eating jam and saltine crackers for several days, with an occasional taste of water to drink, was not forgotten with the smells and sights of the diner. On deck a cooler held the last can of beer. Thirsty, Dick ceremoniously reached in for the beer to celebrate their safe arrival but the can dissolved in his hand; staining the water like weak urine. The salt water had eaten away the aluminum can.

At long last, after agonizing hours of waiting, two well fed, government immigration and customs authorities arrived, checked papers, stamped passports and, before they could leave, Dick and Beverly raced past them to see who could get the first hamburger.

Close on their heels Phil and the Reveille's crew followed them into the small restaurant. The little diner was unprepared to feed six starving and thirsty people at one time. Everything in the diner was quickly consumed; hamburgers, French fries, hot dogs, sandwiches, and the ice tea and lemonade machines drained dry. There was nothing left, the restaurant closed and everyone returned with painfully stuffed but grateful stomachs to the boat for naps.

The next day Dick bought a car, rented a trailer, and helped take the storm shredded sails to a small sail repair shop in town located on a picturesque narrow, tree-lined brick street that seemed more like a New England village. The tiny shop was accustomed to working only on smaller sails, Bimini tops; cushion covers, awnings and miscellaneous canvas repairs. But the Reveille's sails were too large to put in the shop. They were stretched out on the sidewalk in front of the shop, then pulled through the narrow front door, wrestled onto a sewing machine, pulled out the back door and loaded into the trailer when finished. The unusual activity drew a small crowd of curious and amused on-lookers. Dick and Beverly decided it was time to leave. Phil could make the easy, short trip to Cape May without them. That would be the last they would see of the Reveille or her crew.

Not long after Dick saw friends in Titusville, who sailed up from St. Thomas, told him that he and Beverly were lucky to have made it to the states alive. The Reveille when leaving Moorehead City, after her sails were repaired, never made it past the first inlet marker. Her massive center board fell off, she tipped over and sank.

ST. JOAN OF ARC

We do not remember days; we remember moments.

Cesare Pavese

Dick headed back to the islands as quickly as he found a boat going south looking for crew. In St. Croix he met a girl at the Comanche Hotel while waiting to see if he could reconnect with Bishop and renew his associations to export marijuana.

Susanna was traveling with a group of her music students from New York on tour in the US Virgin Islands. She sent them back to the states and agreed to stay for a week when Dick offered to show her around the more interesting places on St. Thomas, besides his apartment at the Mountaintop Hotel with its spectacular view of the Caribbean.

The week went by too quickly. The day she was to leave they walked to town to get some breakfast at the Orange Julius where Sheila's sister worked, then the Post Office to check his mail and from the waterfront they saw a billowing cloud of dense black smoke rising above the buildings. When they got to the waterfront, there was an excited crowd gathered around an island ferryboat that was engulfed in flames and thick diesel smoke.

The old boat was one of a very few boats that provided important inter-island transportation for workers, shoppers and visitors from other islands. Adding fuel to the flames were the now molten plastic curtains and containers of exploding diesel fuel. Rows of fiery wooden benches gave the doomed boat the appearance of an impressive Viking funeral. Then the whole boat suddenly burst into a ball of fire that belched black smoke; depositing black soot over the waterfront, onlookers, visitors and buildings.

The fire station was one block from the burning boat. Attached to the side of Fort Christian the entire station was under frosted corrugated fiber glass roofing that protected the islands two, seldom used, highly polished, and valuable red fire trucks.

Seeing the fire the first truck was quickly dispatched, sirens screaming, to the side of the burning boat. Firemen quickly uncoiled and reeled out the hoses, connected them to the truck, and with hose in hand, nozzle aimed, a signal was given to turn on the water. Standing with feet apart, two firemen braced themselves for the surge of water pressure but only a loud dry hiss of air came out of the hose that sagged limply in his hands. The truck was empty.

Hoses were quickly disconnected, reeled in, coiled on top of the truck, and, with sirens screaming, sped back to the station, got a second truck and with ear-piercing sirens returned to the side of the now completely engulfed boat. Hoses were uncoiled, reeled out, quickly connected to the truck, signal given and this time a gush of water, maybe ten gallons, followed with another loud hiss of air and limp hose. The second truck was also empty.

There was nothing that could be done to save the boat. The nearby pilot boat captain, just returning from guiding a cruise ship into the harbor, saw the smoke and flames. He rushed immediately to the scene, threw a cable over the burning boat's bow and, as the firemen cut the ropes holding the boat to the dock, the pilot towed it out to sea where it could safely burn and sink. When the burning boat swung away from the dock spectators gasped in amusement when they read the boats name, painted in bright red and black letters on its stern, "St. Joan of Ark, Tortola, BVI." It was a sad but fitting end.

TIME TO LEAVE

We must be willing to let go of the life we have planned, so as to accept the life that is waiting for us.

Joseph Campbell

It was 1972. Eight men murdered and robbed at the Fountain Valley Golf Club in St. Croix. A Black Panther had threatened Dick over a drink at the Carousel Bar and a friend's wife was hacked to death by an intruder with a machete last year as she relaxed in her bathtub.

Wayne Aspinall High school students attacked the principal with a beating so bad he was hospitalized for weeks. Not only were physical dangers increasing, there were tensions mounting in the islands delicate racial fabric that had been encouraged by a small group of militant Black Panthers. Paradise was dying. It became apparent to Dick the time was nearing to leave.

During this turbulent time he frequented Fred's bar more often than he was used to and talked fondly about the peaceful days with others who were thinking about weighing anchor and sailing to other islands or returning to the states to escape the depressing disasters unfolding on the island; growing social unrest, violent crimes and invasion of careless, greedy developers.

Dick was tending bar for Fred as a week-end stand-in for one of the new bartenders when Larry Shepherd asked if he would be interested in helping deliver his 110 foot schooner Double Eagle to Fort Lauderdale. He had only met Larry a couple of times and didn't strike him as a particularly competent sailor so it was no surprise that he needed help.

Larry said he needed someone with experience to manage the crew and responsible enough to sail the boat to Florida. He heard about the near disastrous trip Dick made with the Reveille. Without hesitating he agreed to go along on the boat's last two week charter so he could get used to all the lines to handle such a large boat. Shepherd's offer was the cue for him to leave; the moment he sadly knew had to come.

Dick had been an admirer of the graceful 110 foot, Albury built black hulled schooner since her arrival in St. Thomas. She was the ship used in the "Wackiest Ship in The Army," television series; accounting for the costumes and guns under glass in the main salon. The two week charter and trip back to Florida would give him time to think without pressure about what he would do; earnestly consider Louisette's offer and go to Paris, or sail back to find some other island to live on, or go to Washington and camp out on Carol's doorstep or just stay in Lauderdale and work on boats with John. The options were endless but one possibility that could happen had been overlooked.

Reluctantly he told friends Bill, Penny and Louisette of his final decision; maybe he would return to live on Tortola if he could find a boat sailing back from Lauderdale. He would be moving onto the Double Eagle for the next couple of weeks on charter but would see them when he got back and prior to leaving for the states.

The charter party was just boarding when he got to the boat; white nose guards, straw hats, and the smell of coconut lotion decorated two well greased couples from Chicago on their first sailing adventure to the islands; the crew's ship mates for the next seven days.

On board, besides Larry and Barbara Shepherd, was Dick's first mate Al with his girlfriend Lauren; Walter, who was wanted, they found out later, by authorities in Fort Lauderdale, and Alicia. All but Dick, who had his own stateroom, would be housed in the foc'sl crew cabins.

The girls were assigned to help Barbara prepare meals making them exempt from day watch but would take turns taking the night watches on the trip back to the states and make coffee for the night watch.

The first stop was in Road Town Harbor, Tortola to pick up air tanks for a two day dive on the reefs at Bitter End near Virgin Gorda. Several of the guests traveled the first day carefully hanging over the rail; finding little time to enjoy the first day of their trip.

They were anchored for a couple of days of sight seeing, drinking and diving but after experiencing some of Barbara's Portuguese, cold olive oil soaked seafood medley and saltine appetizers, they wisely decided to wait and eat at the Caneel Bay Plantation on St. Johns. After arriving at the Rockefeller resort Dick and Al decided, after taking them ashore, it was time to enjoy several well deserved joints in their absence. Larry and Barbara had enough for the day and went to bed early leaving the crew to be on their own.

Stirring up the ocean's fluorescent creatures for an hour or so with the dinghy, enjoying the luminous spectacle, and smoking plenty of marijuana, they forgot their guests. But first mate Al, who didn't smoke drugs and designated boat operator, rushed the stoned crew back to the boat then to shore to pick up the charter party; all had been tempered by plenty of cocktails and didn't notice the crew's behavior.

Next day the diving tanks were returned to the dive shop in Road Town, the day spent at hurricane hole on St. Johns doing some shallow diving on the remains of an ancient wooden ship. The guests were startled by the unexpected arrival of a large school of barracuda and wisely chose to stay on board for the remainder of the afternoon reading some worn paperback books borrowed from Dick.

From St. Johns they sailed early next morning for a one night stay in Christiansted, St. Croix. Dinner at Ted's Comanche restaurant would be the last meal before heading back to Yacht Haven. With help from several joints, Dick recounted his time spent at the Comanche with Susanna and the night they met Victor Borge; Louisette asking him to go to France; drug smuggling, his favorite story, but the stories depressed him knowing the Double Eagle was now his home until they reached Fort Lauderdale.

Dick was silent as everyone else shared their own memories of living in the islands. It became conversational chaos with some occasional nervous laughter.

The silent, conservative, charter party, was unable to join in the conversation to offer any interesting anecdotes of their own and looked on helplessly, with a touch of disgust, as the crew shared stories of getting stoned, sitting on roof tops to watch the sunrise, smuggling drugs into the island, and how smoking marijuana made for great love making episodes.

After two long weeks the charter party was relieved to finally be back at Yacht Haven Marina fuel dock; the crew said hasty farewells to their sunburned guests, who had cut their charter short by two days to get off the boat and finally get away from Barb's terrible food, engine noise, diesel exhaust, and their dope smoking half crazed crew. No one expected, nor got, the traditional tips.

Preparations were now underway in earnest for the anticipated ten day trip back to the states. Dick didn't want to repeat the mistakes of the Reveille; to be a lost at sea statistic or a victim of an ill prepared boat or end up in the Sargasso Sea. Dick told Larry he felt it best, because of the potential for early summer storms, if they skirt the Bahamas Islands, sail North West skirting the east side of the islands, then turn into Northwest Providence Channel to Florida. If weather got bad or they had an emergency, they could stop in one of several island ports. Larry agreed. The crew gathered around the charts so everyone could see the course Larry and Dick plotted. Leaving in the middle of June was not without its risk.

A storm was brewing over the Yucatan Peninsula of Mexico but they didn't feel as if it would be of any threat since their trip would be east of the Bahamas. If the weather held they would be in Ft. Lauderdale before the storm got that far and if not they would at least be able to duck into an island until the weather improved.

Larry and Barbara made several trips for groceries; bought enough Heineken and Falstaff beer for an around the world cruise in addition to several cases of Mount Gay Rum, and a supply of marijuana from Bill as a farewell gift. Dick made it clear, before leaving that smoking dope and drinking were strictly prohibited when on watch. If caught all alcohol and drugs would be locked up.

The crew of the forty three foot fiberglass sloop Barracuda stopped to visit after hearing of their trip. They were leaving the same day, planned the same course and would stay in radio communication. Larry thought that was a great idea and would make everyone feel a sense of safety knowing someone would be nearby in the event of trouble.

It was the afternoon on the day before they were scheduled to leave. All the provisions had been loaded and Dick was returning to the boat after making a check of the mail at Bob Smith's office. He stopped long enough for a hamburger at the upstairs restaurant and was lost in happy thoughts looking at the stainless steel sink remembering when Jim and he drilled the holes in the ladies shower ceiling.

He stopped, bought a beer, and as he turned to leave a familiar voice from behind, whispered his name so close he felt her breath on his neck. Goose bumps erupted; like a cold chill down his neck and arms. Before he could turn around, she put her arms tightly around him, pressed against his back, clamping his arms helplessly at his sides.

"Guess who," she chirped lightly running her tongue against his neck. This time fairy tale size goose bumps.

He recognized the slight island French accent felt her passionate, lustful embrace he had hoped for when she left him, standing uncomfortably in the water at Morningstar Beach. And now, just like then, that part of him that jumped uncontrollably out of his zipper-less shorts, like a divining rod, was trying it again.

Dick wrestled out of her grip and turned to look at her. He never forgot the voluptuous bare breasted girl of that day at Morningstar. Now he stared at her speechless, his dry mouth open but words would not come out. He was in shock to see how she had changed; not a teenager now. Somewhere behind round cheeks, mounds of firm fleshy breasts, long blond hair, and under yards of loose Jim Tillett fabric, was the new Sheila. Still beautiful and brash in a childish but charming way; she hugged him again then stepped back holding his hands.

"It's good to see you," she said with a soft nervous laughter as she drew a little closer, "where've you been?"

"I had to go back to the states a couple of times. Where've you been? I've been looking for you at the beach since I got back more than a year ago." She firmly gripped his hand with hers; gold rings on each of her fingers felt like he was holding brass knuckles and he was distracted by a small diamond that hung from her left nostril that made little spots of colored lights dance across her cheek when she spoke.

"We moved to St. Vincent but I didn't like it so much and came back a couple of months ago. Remember Morningstar Beach?" She said teasingly. "You still have those shorts?"

"Yeah, but I cut the fly loose. As a matter of fact I got them on now; zipped up." She laughed. More rainbow dots of color flickered across her cheek as she gripped his hand tighter then stood back a little to look at his re-tailored shorts.

"What did you do to them?" She looked puzzled.

"Well, I ripped the seams open and sewed them up with leather boot laces." He turned slightly to show her the sides of his shorts; not tightly sewn revealing that he was not wearing underwear. By the time he got his laundry back, he was used to not wearing any.

"You've got nothing on underneath." She sounded slightly surprised but not shocked and moved closer. His shorts were getting tighter.

"I'm getting ready to sail this boat to Fort Lauderdale tomorrow," Dick said nervously pointing with his free hand at the Double Eagle.

He started walking slowly towards the boat with Sheila pressed tightly against his side, holding his hand; her free hand gripped his elbow; her closeness creating a desperate, painful struggle in his cut-offs.

"It's too bad," she said with a frown, "that you're leaving just when I get to see you again. My mom and sister are still in St. Vincent and they remember you."

Dick didn't ask how they remembered him. He remembered too well meeting her mother at the Carousel Bar, the cigarette stuck to his lip, the burns in the crotch of his finger, the drool of anticipation and how her mom quickly herded them away from him.

"Can I go on board?" She asked cautiously, "I've never

been on a boat like this and I might never see you again."

Dick had a feeling he was getting close to his Morningstar dream. "This is going to be great sex," he thought.

"Sure. I don't think anyone will mind," He struggled not to sound too excited. It was difficult because he felt what was coming next or at least he hoped. He was powerless to stop, "and we do have a little time before we leave." His throat was Sahara desert dry; voice cracked. Dick all but pushed her down below, grabbed and, not wanting to waste time, opened two beers as they rushed through the galley and into the main salon.

Below, Barbara was sitting comfortably next to his stateroom reading. He nervously introduced her to Sheila, showed her quickly around the boat and the crew's quarters, telling her about the movies the boat had been in before coming to St. Thomas and where they had been recently on charter.

"And this is my stateroom," he said passing Barbara who quickly excused herself then went topside, "and as you can see there's just enough room for me and my books." He turned and proudly waved his free hand over the collection of his books on the shelf.

When he turned around Sheila had closed the door and, with fewer motions than it took him to drop his shorts, she was standing there wearing only her gold jewelry. Between them only two pieces of clothing lying in a small pile at her feet. In spite of her added weight, she was still beautiful. She had reappeared in a blaze of delicious memories of that hot afternoon when she swam over to him at Morningstar Beach but this time without distractions; his old fantasy fulfilled.

When he woke up exhausted, she was gone but left some small trinkets for him on the shelf next to his bunk; a tiny vial of her perfume, a small gold ring and a jar of sand and note with one word written on it, Morningstar.

Lauren and Alicia were in the main salon outside the stateroom pretending to read a Cosmopolitan magazine when he opened the door.

"You know," he said almost proudly, "I've been waiting years for that moment since I first saw her."

They looked at him, smiling. He decided it was probably best not to say more and went to Fred's bar hoping Sheila would be somewhere close but she was gone. He was ready to leave now; memories were made complete.

Water Island disappeared behind St. Thomas as they sailed past Sail Rock and into the Virgin Passage. Behind them the Barracuda was preparing to leave later in the day making her less than a day behind.

Until reaching the Northwest Providence Passage at Eluthera Island, ten days later, the trip was uneventful. Sharks had bitten off several of the taff-rail log spinners leaving only a rudimentary way of determining speed by throwing bits of paper off the bow and time how long it took to travel the length of the boat.

Nothing had been heard from the Barracuda in days and with no distress calls everyone assumed all was well. The weather was beginning to deteriorate rapidly with high winds and seas making a reefed main necessary. By the time they reached the West side of the Northwest Passage the strong winds forced them to further reduce sail by furling in the inner jib, and reduce the main to a second reef.

The storm was Hurricane Agnes that had skipped across the Gulf and Florida rapidly and had become one of the earliest and largest of the season. It was the tropical depression that formed over the Yucatan Peninsula in Mexico as they left St. Thomas and its rapid movement was unexpected. Once across Florida, it developed into the storm they were sailing into. Without a radio they were unable to receive weather advisories and thought it was a nothing more than a typical summer storm that commonly occurs near the Gulf Stream.

It was early morning when they spotted a few shimmering lights from the Florida coast. Unsure of where they were Larry wisely decided to stay at sea until daylight when they could get close enough for a visual on a landmark to determine where they were. As the day brightened, the seas became more worked up, the winds increased, and several towers were spotted allowing them to plot their position; they were just outside the Palm Beach Shores Inlet.

As they motored through the inlet and into the channel, the boat shuddered and came to an unexpected, abrupt stop. Larry had ignored the chart, put the 175 ton boat hard into the mud just off Peanut Island and then sheared the coupling bolts off the shaft when trying to dislodge the boat from the mud.

With the help of the Coast Guard Auxiliary, who warned they were impeding traffic by being anchored in the channel, they managed to get the necessary bolts, make the repairs, and finally move the boat into a safer anchorage.

Dick and the crew, while Larry was making the repairs, jumped ship without clearing Customs or Immigration, and rowed ashore to a local bar for some welcome cold beer and hamburgers. The next day began with high winds and seas but they were determined to get to Fort Lauderdale in spite of the weather. Fortunately the storm had crossed Florida to the North but the winds and seas plagued them until they reached Fort Lauderdale thirty six hours later but they had missed the worst of the storm.

Rain drops driven by the high winds made stinging welts on their arms forcing them to wear dive masks to protect their eyes. The boat plunged deep burying her bow into the high ocean waves; sea water swept over the boat from bow to stern forcing the need for canvas to be nailed over the skylights and forward hatches to prevent taking on more water than the bilge pumps could handle.

To avoid sailing head long into the rougher seas of the Gulf Stream, they were dangerously close to shore. Suddenly the helm spun free and lost control of the boats rudder when the steering cable broke. Dick called everyone on deck to furl all sails. The main sail was sheeted in to keep the boat headed into the wind and waves until the steering was restored. The emergency tiller was useless. The deck fitting was corroded shut and couldn't be opened to get to the rudder post so the emergency tiller could be attached. The weather was pushing them closer to shore and if beached in such heavy seas the boat would be destroyed and their lives in danger.

Alan, Dick's first mate, went below to fix the broken cable because he was the only one small enough to slide under the dangerously swinging quadrant. He came back on deck smiling. A couple of cable clamps fixed the problem and steering was restored. Sails were unfurled, reefed and the thirty-six mile stormy voyage to Fort Lauderdale resumed. After two days fighting high seas and winds, they cheered as they sailed into the calm waters of Port Everglades.

They pulled alongside the Marina del American's dock, threw lines to waiting hands, plugged into shore power, and all was secured.

The Double Eagle was impounded by Customs. Being illegally registered as a foreign vessel made everyone on board guilty of piracy. Larry had changed the boats registration, a U.S. Documented vessel, to the British Virgin Islands without first getting the approval of the U.S. Department of Transportation. That, by definition, constitutes piracy under US Maritime law. For the first time since living in the islands and being involved in other nefarious activities, Dick was now accused of piracy after doing nothing more than helping deliver a boat. His résumé was nearly complete.

Epilogue

And in the end, it's not the years in your life that count. It's the life in your years.

Abraham Lincoln

The British and US Virgin Islands in the Caribbean was the paradise to enjoy of the 60's and 70's. Passports, Visas and other documents were unnecessary for island to island travel; come and go as you please. Everyone was welcome.

Adventurers used the islands as a base of operations for drug smuggling or as a springboard for South American legal and not so legal activities. There were treasure hunters, counterfeiters, assassins, Black Panthers, rock stars, movie stars, wealthy industrialists, and lots of other folks looking to escape into a world removed from their boring and ordinary lives. Others brought their yachts to join the large charter fleet in St. Thomas or stop to visit before continuing on to other ports.

The islands would enter into a frenzy of violent crime

and unchecked development in the 70's that would change forever the peaceful, free, frontier paradise.

Native fishing schooners disappeared; high speed hydrofoil ferries replaced colorful native ferries; a mega yacht luxury marina was built on the bones of the old Yacht Haven Marina and Fred's Frigorific Fraternity Bar, where the stories in this book had their beginning; the place where many people began and some ended their adventures. It was a way of life that opened the doors of real life adventure and inspired the short stories of Caribbean Bones.

The ghosts of Yacht Haven and its Marina still haunt me but in a good way.

Not a day passes that I don't remember sharing a drink and laugh with Mama Cass; playing darts with "Mad Dog," Fairchild on Virgin Gorda; liars' poker with actor Bill Davis at Trader Dan's on the waterfront or, "The Lovin' Spoonful," my stoned rock band neighbors at Yacht Haven Marina. I went to the islands to find adventure and explore the wonders of freedom and found more than I had ever hoped for.

Now, remembering what it was like then, I was looking out of the planes window with watery eyes as Sail Rock came into view in the distance. It was the first island I saw when I arrived years ago.

The stories in Caribbean Bones are what I call, "Faction;" a lot of fact blended with a little bit of fiction. I continue to sail to the islands each year and find it difficult to see the unrelenting changes; forgetting that today it will be someone else's paradise in a world they live in that begins on a cruise ship.

Made in the USA
Charleston, SC
07 February 2012